"You and I are going to drive to Peter's house," I shouted with ecstasy. "You are going to zap him with a poisoned arrow and I'm going to live happily ever after!"

Love, he ranted, isn't all it's drummed up to be, *especially* if we don't know the other person well at all, *especially* if we're crazy about a person just because of how they look! I assured him that how Peter looked was only a minuscule part of why I was mad about him.

He eyed me wearily. "Infatuation cannot be sustained indefinitely, my friend. Love that embraces the entire person is a monumental gift that takes time to grow!"

"I don't have time to grow! The King of Hearts Dance is six days away, and I'm going! I'm going with Peter Terris because you're going to shoot him, Jonathan!"

I grabbed my car keys, flung on my black bomber jacket, and headed to my Volvo and destiny.

JOAN BAUER is a freelance writer who has worked in advertising, radio, television, and film. Her first novel for young adults, *Squashed*, was a *School Library Journal* Best Book of the Year and winner of the Delacorte Press Prize for a First Young Adult Novel. Born in River Forest, Illinois, Joan Bauer now lives in Darien, Connecticut, with her husband, daughter, and assorted animals.

Thwonk

JOAN BAUER

Published by
Bantam Doubleday Dell Books for Young Readers
a division of
Bantam Doubleday Dell Publishing Group, Inc.
1540 Broadway
New York, New York 10036

ISBN 0-440-21980-9

RL: 7.2
Reprinted by arrangement with Delacorte Press

Printed in the United States of America
June 1996
10 9 8 7 6 5
OPM

For Jean,
who always believed

Thwonk

CHAPTER ONE

I was in my makeshift darkroom above the garage developing my umpteenth print of Peter Terris, an individual of full-orbed gorgeousness who needs absolutely no retouching, an individual oozing with classic tones and highlights who barely knew that I was alive. I had taken this shot in great diffused light in the Benjamin Franklin High School Student Center, catching Peter poised perfectly by the sainted statue of Big Ben himself. I had taken it from afar (distance being the basic glitch in our relationship), using my ace Nikon F2 and zoom lens while hiding behind a fake marble pillar. I was hiding because if he knew I'd been secretly photographing him for all these months he would think I was immature, neurotic, and obsessive.

I'm not.

I'm an artist.

Artists are always misunderstood.

My red safelight shot a warm glow through my darkroom. I sloshed developer solution around the photographic paper (sloshing was a key developing technique) and rocked the tray gently as Peter's face filled the paper. At first it was hazy like a shadow, then the fine grains appeared and flowed into chiseled sensation. I dipped the paper in fixing solution to stop the process, rinsed it, ran a squeegee over it, and hung it on a clothesline to dry. I studied the photograph and felt my kidneys curl. It was a surprising shot that caught you off guard, like seeing an old friend unexpectedly. My father, who taught me everything he knew about photography, would call it "a decisive moment." It dripped emotion like a great photograph should.

I pushed back my swivel chair and sighed deeply.

I have spent the last five months trying not to love him.

I sneezed with emotion, being a chronic allergy sufferer, whipped out my nasal inhaler, and gave each nostril a long, tormented squirt.

Falling in love is a massive pain.

I locked the darkroom door and slumped through my studio. It was February sixth: eight days until Valentine's Day. I was dateless, as usual, deep in the vice grip of unrequited love.

It was bad enough not having a boyfriend for New Year's Eve. Now I had to cope with Valentine datelessness, feeling consummate social pressure from every retailer in America who stuck hearts and cupids in their windows by January second to rub it in.

There was the humiliation of not having a date to the King of Hearts Dance at school, a dance considered by persons in the know to be an excellent way to get a date to the prom if you weren't otherwise attached, a dance that is held every Valentine's Day in the Benjamin Franklin High School Student Center in a massive celebration of teenage romance and universal love. I started down the garage steps that led from my studio and nearly tripped over Stieglitz, my dog, a forty-pound black-and-white keeshond (pronounced caze-hawnd) fur ball named for Alfred Stieglitz, great black-and-white photographer of the turn of the century. He lunged at me with unbridled glee because the mere sight of my presence always made his day. It's important to have a dog. Dogs love unconditionally.

I knelt down to pat him. "Have you ever noticed, Stieglitz, that love is filled with pain and torture and promises nothing but agony?"

Stieglitz hadn't noticed, wagged his tail, and tried

to climb into my lap. I crashed through the garage, into the kitchen, and contemplated my dilemma.

The whole thing with Peter Terris started five months ago, and I'd like to say from the outset that I wasn't looking for trouble. I was walking through the Student Center to English Lit, speed-reading *Beowulf,* when I tripped over Peter's flawless foot and crashed at his feet like a complete spaz. I would have written the whole thing off to consummately bleak timing had I not gazed into his ice-green eyes, observed that they were positively riveting, and frozen in time. This was hazardous. I was trying to avoid eye contact with the entire male species. My last relationship had just crumbled and left me emotionally blotto when Todd Kovich, my boyfriend of four gut-wrenching months, left to attend Yale University, and spoke those parting words favored by churls and two-timers the world over:

"I'll call you."

Did he call?

Have I heard one syllable from him since August twenty-third?

Do pigs fly?

So there I was, flopped at Peter Terris's feet, still reeling from Todd's premier abandonment. I brushed myself off. I reminded myself that falling for another gorgeous guy was beyond stupid, particularly when that guy was captain of the varsity soccer team and going out with Julia Hart, who was excruciatingly beautiful or, as my best friend, Trish Beckman, put it, "Death Incarnate." Nothing could pry a male from Julia Hart's side with the possible exception of a blowtorch.

I smiled and tried to exit gracefully, and instead I managed to half-trip. Peter Terris was looking at me like a child watches a clown in the circus. I limped off. That's when Trish Beckman accosted me by the World Peace Bench that had been given to the school by last year's graduating class. Trish is in the Drama Guild and reacts theatrically to everything.

"Don't even think about Peter Terris, A.J.!" she snarled.

I held up my hands in innocence.

"It's not going to work," Trish railed. "I saw the whole thing. Your eyes got gooey." She examined my hands and shook her head. "Your hands are sweaty." She lowered her voice ominously to a stage whisper. "We've seen this before."

No joke. Trish and I have been best friends since sixth grade and we've been through everything together —countless romantic devastations, the constant attacks of her little brat brother, plus the epic horror of her father's midlife crisis when he wore skintight shirts and called everybody "Babe."

"*Say it!*" Trish demanded.

"I am not going to fall for the wrong guy again," I mumbled.

She studied my face.

I rubbed my eyes. "I'm fine," I assured her.

That was five months ago. I wasn't fine then and I'm not fine now.

Let's talk tragedy.

I've had four, count them, four boyfriends with definite dream potential turn into Swiss cheese in one year. Two went back to their old girlfriends, one insulted my photography, and Todd, saphead that he is, graduated and went to Yale. I've missed one prom ("Let's Keep the Magic Forever"), last year's Homecoming Howl, and the King of Hearts Dance three years running.

I have dating strengths, you understand. I am not ugly. I have long chestnut hair, solid brown eyes, excellent teeth, and a small nose I can wrinkle if I have to. I am tall (almost five nine), slim, except for my knees which will probably pudge out by the time I hit thirty. I have less of a waist than I'd like, less of a chin than I'd like, but I wear clothes well and I can handle minor repairs on any car without seeming overbearing.

My parents are concerned about how quickly I fall in love.

"Why do you think, A.J.," they say in unison, "that you find these boys so attractive?"

I didn't say that this fiery chemical explosion leaps from somewhere inside me. Parents don't want to hear these things. I shrugged and said nothing.

"Maybe you should try sitting on the intensity,"

Mom suggests, "just until your feelings catch up with reality."

"We could chain you to the water heater," Dad offers, "until these little moments pass."

You see what I'm up against.

I've tried expressing my love life photographically —the smashed Orange Crush can lying in the middle of an empty playground is my favorite. I'll be thinking I'm doing fine and then I see a couple float down the street, massively in love, and I remember being that way, even though it was fleeting. I remember feeling wanted and desirable and important and then the sadness comes crashing in and I review every guy who dumped me, all the way back to Marty Michler who laughed at the cupid Valentine I gave him in fourth grade and showed it to everyone at recess.

If you want to really know me you have to look at my photography, because my art and I are intrinsically tied. I was seven years old when photography and I collided in Italy. I looked through the viewfinder of my father's Leica at the Leaning Tower of Pisa, tilted the camera until the Tower stood razor straight, and snapped. When the prints came back I was hooked by the power of a small machine that could fix a falling building. Dad bought me my own used 35mm, and I set out to capture all of life honestly through my lens.

Guys don't understand great art. They don't care that sometimes the camera has power beyond the photographer to record emotion that only the heart can see. They're threatened when the camera jumps ahead of me. Todd Kovich was ripped when I brought my F2 to the prom, but I'd missed too many transcendent shots over the years to ever take a chance of missing one again. A prom, I told him, had a boundless supply of photogenic bozos who could be counted on to do something base.

Few males appreciate the role of the artist in a crumbling world. But I held out great hope for Peter Terris.

I was standing at the kitchen door watching my father work. Dad was in another world, holding two boxes of ChocoMallowChunks cereal—the cherished new product of his biggest client, ChocoChunks International— holding them like a weary father would cradle newborn twins. He was carving out a new ad campaign and reaching into the core of his creative volcano to find something important to say about a children's breakfast cereal that contained enough refined sugar to seriously alter a generation's SAT scores. I thought about clearing my voice to let him know I was there. I thought about the hurt of the last few months that kept crashing in around us.

I leaned against the door silently as Dad gripped the cereal boxes and exhaled slowly, bonding with the product. This was how he taught me to approach photography: "Entwine yourself with the subject," Dad often said, "until its essence floods your being." This was not always easy, but when I connected it was magic and I have the awards to prove it. I won the "Most Textural" ribbon at the Crestport Arts and Oyster Festival with my searing still life "Bowl of Bean Dip"; I cinched the coveted Northeast FotoFast Youth Photography Contest with "Tootsies," my socko close-up of Betsy Manero's brother's toes.

Dad slapped the counter. "We're going full bore!" he announced to the air. "Major PR all across America to announce the new cereal flavor. ChocoMallowChunks awards to young athletes. We'll put their pictures on the box, highlight their families, how their parents got up before dawn for eight years to get them to the pool, ice rink, whatever. Poor slobs. We'll get contests going in schools—the winners get parties with rock groups, the kids become local heroes. T-shirts, visors, chocolate iridescent scratch-and-smell stickers. We'll saturate America with coupon madness!"

Dad stepped back, satisfied, as the kitchen clock tolled. He was a smidgen over six feet tall, dark and swarthy with an on-again, off-again mustache. Advertising is Dad's second incarnation. He'd struggled as an independent filmmaker and sometime photographer for eleven cash-poor years, and came *so close* to making it. But each project went bust—budgets were obliterated, minds were changed, his photos almost sold. "Almost," as Dad says, "doesn't pay the rent." He cut bait on my sixth birthday, bought a suit, and "went commercial." I hated that suit. He wore it like it was heavy armor for fighting dragons. I think he was battling more than he knew.

Dad took what he knew about filmmaking and went into advertising, where he has been very successful. He's made Topper's toiletbowl brushes dance with soul, turned Sparky's toothbrushes into jet-propelled purple lasers, pitted Zitslayer acne gel against vampire pimples, and coaxed a chorus of EasyOn panty hose to sing like they really meant it. This is a person who can squeeze meaning from a stone.

He can also be obtuse.

When I made my ultimate announcement last November that I was going to be an artist, go to arts college, make my name in photography, Dad hit the roof. "A career in the arts has no security, A.J.," he barked. "You will walk the streets alone, be kicked in the stomach time and again by cretins who have no clue as to what you're trying to say. No daughter of mine is going to throw her life away!"

He stormed off with me shouting that we needed to discuss it and him shouting back that there was nothing to discuss. Mom tried to step in and make peace like she always does, but the battle lines had been drawn. That's when the Wall went up between us—part silence, part pain. We've been like two porcupines passing in a narrow hallway ever since.

So I sent my college applications off to the "right schools," the ones according to Dad that would give me the "right education," praying they'd all hate me. And with my mother's guarded permission I sent my finest photographic work off to several superior arts schools, not knowing what would happen if they accepted me. One night I saw Dad slumped in the family room staring at my first self-portrait (I was twelve) like he was hypnotized. I so wanted to ask him, "Do you think I have enough talent to make it, Dad?"

I didn't ask him though.

Dad said when I got my first camera I arranged my shots with the controlling passion of a football coach calling the plays. I categorically deny this. Okay, so once or twice I pulled my parents apart when they were having one of their epic fights that happened after we first moved to Connecticut when Mom had to leave her catering business behind in Chicago because Dad had taken a big-muck advertising position in Manhattan and wasn't around very much.

"All right, Mommy and Daddy," I announced. "Hug each other and smile at the camera."

Hugging didn't help. What really helped was when I fell out of the big oak tree in the front yard and broke my arm. Mom and Dad were in marriage counseling then trying to rechannel their anger, but they stopped being angry quick at the pitiful sight of me screaming for mercy in the emergency room. I am allergic to pain. By the time the cast came off they were cuddling and listening to jazz like the old days. I took a photograph of the cast (my first still life) and gave it to them on their anniversary. Mom cried when she saw it; Dad sniffed proudly and said it stood for brokenness and remembering what was important. It just goes to show you the eternal power of capturing a moment in time.

My biggest fear in life, along with drying up romantically, is not making it with my photography. When Dad and I used to take our cameras and go looking for pictures together, like we did over the summer —pounding the streets of New York City, shooting roll after roll of Fifth Avenue shoppers and broken-down taxis—I wanted to hug him and tell him how sorry I am that his passion can't be his career.

"It's my hobby now," Dad insisted, "and that's enough."

If that happens to me, if I can't make the world listen to what I have to say through my art, I think I'll die.

Dad was staring at the boxes of ChocoMallowChunks cereal like they held the secrets to the universe. His phone rang; that's when he noticed me.

I coughed. "Hi . . ."

Dad looked down and shoved his hands in his pockets. "I need to get the phone," he muttered.

"Right."

I flopped on the overstuffed kitchen couch and watched him go. I wondered what would happen to all his films and photographs in the upstairs closet—the documentaries on homelessness and drug addiction, the funny short subjects, the half-finished romantic comedy, the boxes of slice-of-life photographs that speak volumes about the human condition. I wondered how you stop caring about what you've ached over, sweated over. I wondered if my father would ever trust me as an artist. I wondered if Peter Terris even knew I was alive.

I focused my F2 on a Valentine candy heart lying forlornly by the sink; warm light washed over it. I ate half the heart to add brokenhearted realism, and was standing on a stool for an aerial view when the phone rang, the answering machine clicked on.

"I hope," said Pearly Shoemaker's voice, "that you're working on the Valentine cover shot, A.J. . . ." She paused here for effect. Pearly was the angst-ridden editor of the Benjamin Franklin High School *Oracle,* the school paper where I toiled day and night as the principal photographer for absolutely no money. "Since," she continued, "the rest of the edition can't go to press without it! An edition I've been slaving over for six months!" I closed my eyes; I knew she wasn't done. "If you're *not* working on it, A.J., *we're all finished!*"

I moved in close with my macro lens for a broad, cartoon feel and clicked off three fast shots of the Valentine heart with half its life gone.

"I'm working on it!" I growled.

"I know you're there, A.J.!" She said this snarling and hung up.

I should have known better than to ever get involved in this lame assignment. The Valentine edition was to be the biggest thing to hit love and high-school journalism since graffiti.

"I can see it!" Pearly had shouted, when she first approached me with the idea. "An entire edition about love and those tumultuous teenage years. It'll be hundreds of pages, we'll market it to local businesses—everyone will buy an ad, A.J., because who can say no to love? I'll . . . I mean, *we'll* be famous!" She went on to say that the *Oracle,* normally free, would be selling on Valentine's Day for two dollars, cold cash, no credit, and for that the A. J. McCreary cover shot had to be perfect.

I groaned.

"Just do it, A.J.!" she snarled.

I've shot weird scenes through dark, murky filters, teenage couples hugging out of focus, a boy and girl kissing outside Petrocelli's Poultry as Mr. Petrocelli hung two seven-pound roasters in the window. Pearly wanted something advertisers could relate to.

"Think Valentine's Day, A.J.! Hearts, cupids . . . !"

"I don't do cupids, Pearly. They're trite."

"Couples holding hands . . ."

"Primitive . . ."

"*Nothing weird!*" she shrieked. "*Nothing depressing! And absolutely nothing oblique or obscure!*"

"*What's left?*" I yelled it.

"*Normal,* A.J. *Normal* is left!"

I don't do normal. I have a reputation to uphold.

So I kept combing the streets of Crestport, Connecticut, looking for the essence of love to shoot when my own heart was ground into farina. I saw gray slushy sidewalks and February skies. I saw a little boy punch his sister in the stomach. I saw irritated shoppers, perfectly sculpted evergreens, and then I saw my worst nightmare—Peter Terris and Julia Hart walking hand in hand across Mariah Boulevard looking positively photogenic, oblivious to the winter muck clinging to their designer shoes. Peter brushed a strand of hair off Julia's face and kissed her pink nose. Julia nuzzled his shoulder like a lovesick kitten. They floated past me, the Perfect Teenage Couple, oozing Valentine's Day passion and *Oracle* cover potential.

I turned from the hated scene drowning in waves of sadness and sank behind an evergreen in epic despair.

CHAPTER TWO

"What," I whispered to my mother, *"could possibly happen in forty-eight hours?"*

Mom gave me a we'll-talk-about-this-later-but-since-you-asked, *a-lot*-could-happen look from behind the counter at the Emotional Gourmet. We'd been back and forth for weeks about whether I could survive alone in the house for forty-eight hours while my parents went to a gourmet convention in New Orleans. The fact that I was going to be eighteen in thirty-six days, moments away from consummate adulthood, had no impact. They were leaving tonight and from all the angst, you would have thought they were dropping me and Stieglitz from a biplane onto an ice floe to survive by our wits until they returned. Mom adjusted the red satin Valentine heart above the cash register that matched the hanging heartlettes over the door, and nudged me forward to wait on the next customer. It was Saturday morning and the shop was packed, as usual.

Mrs. T. Alexander Worthington ordered one dozen of Mom's famous sautéed cashew buns; I put them into an eco-conscious brown bag, grinning in true gourmet style, because Mrs. Worthington was the richest woman in town and expected to be catered to. "That's twelve dollars," I said.

She blistered: *"I have an account, dear!"* Rich people never carry money.

I kept smiling because Mrs. Worthington was Mom's best customer and extolled Mom's gastronomic virtues to everyone she knew in the Tri-State area. I wrote her order in the charge account book: *Old Bat/ Twelve bucks.* Mom glared at me and slapped the book shut.

The fabulous smells of hot white chocolate and Mom's perfect cinnamon rolls wafted through the store. There is something primordial about happiness and food and Mom's shop plays right into it. The counters bulged with her Saturday creations: mozzarella and prosciutto bread, fat caramel biscuits, pesto-stuffed raviolis, roasted pork with brandied apples. Mom always says that great food should massage the senses.

Sonia, the plump store manager and resident grandmother, gobbled a butterscotch brownie, wailing that she'd be a size eight if she worked someplace else. Hal Blitzer, Mom's partner, bowed grandly to the next woman in line. Mom put dense cheddar bread into a bag for a man who said this was his wife's favorite—he'd driven all the way from New Jersey to buy it because today was their anniversary. Several women in the store jabbed their husbands on hearing this. I hung my head —Peter Terris wouldn't cross the street to buy me a Twinkie.

Mom smiled big and wide and handed the man a yellow rose from the vase of flowers she kept by the cash register for special occasions. No one treats her customers better than Christine McCreary, ace chef and businessperson of the century.

My mother has the Touch. She knows what flowers go with what occasions, what hors d'oeuvres work with what people. She believes passionately in the power of food to heal, restore, and stimulate relationships, and she has built a following of loyal customers who really hope she's right. If she's wrong, says Sonia, no one wants to know.

Moving to Crestport was hard for Mom. She'd had a smattering of hard-earned catering success in Chicago, and found herself starting from scratch in a sleepy little town that didn't much care for outsiders and didn't know the difference between a *cornichon* and a kielbasa. Mom watched the pace of Crestport, Connecticut, from the sidelines, trying to determine her role. Three months later she marched into Hal Blitzer's gourmet shop on Seminole Avenue and announced that she could bring him untold business by giving cooking classes to the locals.

Hal Blitzer's eyebrows shot up. "What kinds of classes?"

"Indian lunches, Italian barbecues, Bistro Breakfasts, Amazing Gourmet Baby Foods. Can I be frank?"

"Please."

"Crestport women are *bored.* They need excitement, nourishment, emotional bedding. If you turn them on to new foods they can prepare themselves, new avenues in which to entertain and amaze their friends, they will count on you for everything, Mr. Blitzer!"

"Call me Hal."

Mom began cooking classes one month later, after lavish advertising created by Dad in the *Crestport Crier:* "Wrap yourself in the emotions of food!" the ads declared, and Crestport women *did,* along with a decent cross-section from neighboring New Leonard and the southern tip of Stanwich. I came by every day after school, did my homework in the office, and watched the great culinary drama unfold at my mother's feet. By my ninth birthday Hal Blitzer had tripled his floor space, and Christine McCreary, the Emotional Gourmet, was firmly rooted in New England sod. In three years she became Hal Blitzer's full-fledged partner.

This was not without pain.

The hours are abhorrent. The people are demanding. The equipment is heavy. But Mom is called to the food business like an artist is called to a canvas. Mom believes there is a flash of brilliance in every person. Dad says she'd change her mind if she had to ride the subway every day.

I've worked with Mom for years, and like all chef's children I've been called upon to perform bizarre tasks —delivering four hundred boxed dinners in a monsoon when the service crew got lost, rinsing lettuce for three hundred in the Maytag (forty seconds on Delicate) when the salad lady saw a mouse in the kitchen and fainted. Mom says it takes a person with lightning-quick reflexes to handle the big gourmet traumas. I say it helps when you believe in your mother's vision and she pays quite decently above minimum wage. In third grade we had to write an essay on one of the important things our mothers taught us. I entitled mine "Never Trust a Linen Service." Mom had it plasticized and keeps it in her desk drawer.

Being a chef, my mother's downfall is food fixation. She can lose sleep about weaving salmon and swordfish into a braid. She can kill an evening hurling spun sugar onto a towel rack. She can yell at me for not cutting meat on an angle and criticize the way I tie the string on a bakery box. That *really* frosts me. She could, as she was doing now, rearrange an antipasto platter that *I* had designed, and fixate on the aesthetic placement of the Calamata olives . . .

"Christine," whispered Sonia, taking her arm, "the olives look very special where they are."

They did too.

Mom made her *Hmmmmm* sound, which meant she wouldn't be happy with it even if the Calamata olives did backflips, and relinquished the antipasto. She was tired, waging her constant battle between busyness and rest. Mom loves the business, but feels guilty about the long hours she spends at work and compares herself too often with other mothers who are always around for breakfast.

"I'm nothing like the other mothers!" she wails.

I nod.

"Do you feel deprived, A.J., because we never did little sewing projects together?"

"You can't sew, Mom."

"I never painted stencils of ballerinas in your bedroom!"

"I'm sure that's why I can't get a decent date, Mother. Ballerina stencils would have turned the tide for me, but it's too late now . . ."

That's when Mom will usually throw a potholder at me and stop feeling guilty. Once I overheard her telling Sonia, "I'm afraid that if I slow down, it will all go away."

We worked into the late afternoon as we always did on Saturdays—slicing bread, bagging orders, kissing up to demanding customers. It takes big lips to succeed in this business. By five o'clock the crowds had thinned and Mom was arranging the food that was left into smaller bowls. Abundance at all cost, even at closing.

I was packing goodies for the weekly food baskets that Mom sends to the homeless shelter in New Leonard. Every Christmas she joins forces with Crestport Congregational Church—she pudges Dad up as Santa, me as an elf, and throws a party at the shelter with roast beef and turkey and everything in between. She has a sign in her office: TO WHOM MUCH IS GIVEN, MUCH IS REQUIRED. Mom doesn't preach much about helping others, she just goes and does it.

I don't know what the world will be like when I get older; I hope it gets better, but it really might not. I worry about my future on a planet with so many problems. Crestport seems unreal to me sometimes. We have so much here; we take our privileges for granted. Mom never bought into the ease of this town. That's made her something of an outsider.

Like me.

Mom was julienning broccoli that hadn't sold to use for tomorrow's garnish. Her hair was done up in a french braid that made her face look longer. Her glasses were smudged as usual, which hid the darkness of her eyes. She wore a sunshine-yellow apron that brought out the highlights of her auburn hair.

"I just wish, sweetie," Mom said, "that you were going to stay with Trish while your dad and I are gone."

That again. I said what she already knew, that Stieglitz would have to go to a kennel because Trish's little brother, Devon, is allergic to everything and Stieglitz would sulk in abject devastation for days. I said that Stieglitz would terrorize any bad guys who came to the door.

"What, Mother, could possibly happen in forty-eight hours?"

She chose not to answer.

"I'll strap a fire extinguisher on my back and lug around the mobile phone, okay?"

"Even when you sleep . . ." she insisted.

I put my hand over my heart. "So help me, Mom, I'll look so weird, no one will come near me."

"That's my girl."

Mom stifled a yawn and touched the laugh lines around her mouth like she was trying to erase them. Time was her relentless foe. She was up at four most mornings to begin food preparation, asleep by nine each night. The added tension between Dad and me rankled everyone.

"Talk to Dad," I pleaded. "Try to get him to understand."

Mom sighed. "I've talked to him, A.J. I've talked

to you. Nothing is going to happen, my darling, until the two of you talk to each other."

"He's not being fair!"

"It's complicated, honey. He's frightened for you."

"You're taking his side now?" I slammed blueberry preserves into the food basket.

"I am *not*," she countered wearily. A buzzer went off in the kitchen. Mom threw up her hands and ran back to check it.

I slumped on the counter exhausted. The day was only beginning for me. I had agreed to cover the Ben Franklin High School Piranhas basketball game tonight for the *Oracle,* and it would behoove me to get some decent action shots, or Pearly Shoemaker would have a musk ox on my lawn. I reached my weary arms to the ceiling and did a full body stretch. I did jumping jacks and felt my strength return . . .

That's when the glass-etched double doors of the Emotional Gourmet opened and Peter Terris sauntered in.

I froze in midjack.

There he was, in extreme wonderfulness, wearing a red sweater and jeans and a blue ski jacket—walking under Mom's hanging red satin Valentine hearts! Walking right toward me!

"I need a pie," he said.

I slammed my arms to my sides and hit the floor. *"We have those . . . !"*

"You do aerobics here?" he asked, laughing.

I caught my breath and wiped sweat on my sunshine-yellow apron. "I was trying to wake up," I muttered. I lunged toward the pie case: *"Pies,"* I said lustily.

Not much was left, because it was the end of a busy day. This was awful, since he'd come all the way here to get a pie. It took twelve minutes from his house —I knew this—I'd made the trip many times, just to drive by. He could have gone to Munson's Bakery, which was closer to his house. He'd *never* set one perfect foot in Mom's store before, to my knowledge, and now here he was.

This meant he cared!

We stood together, sharing oxygen, in front of the pie case. I didn't want him to leave disappointed, unless the pie was for Julia Hart.

"What kind have you got?" Peter asked. My heart was pounding, my hands were shaking. I looked at the pie case and lost all familiarity with the English language.

"Uh . . . there's . . . uh . . ." I tried pointing.

"Apple?" he asked. I nodded. He shook his surfer-sandy hair. "My mother wants something unusual."

His mother! That was safe. She must be a wonderful person. I smiled deeply. He pointed at the other pie, a strawberry rhubarb piled with whipped cream.

"That one," he said.

I took the luckiest pie in the world from the case and didn't drop it. I tied it up expertly and had to cut the string because I'd wrapped it around my watch. I had a mild allergy attack at the cash register as Peter looked around, whistling. I wanted to say that it took a special person to pick out a strawberry rhubarb pie. I wanted to say that I hoped he really enjoyed it and there were plenty more where that came from. I took his money; our thumbs touched.

"Thanks," he said, smiling.

"Thank *you*," I said. Thank you for making my entire weekend. Thank you for being gorgeous beyond words. I watched him go and spent a few moments leaning against the pie case containing one common apple pie that had always been my favorite, till now. I breathed in the air that Peter Terris had breathed.

"Well," said my mother, appearing from the back, "was that a friend of yours?"

I snapped to attention. "Just a guy at school . . ." I said nonchalantly. I Windexed the pie case to preserve it.

"He's cute," said Mom.

I said "I guess . . ." and wiped down the cash register that didn't need it.

It was night; 10:03 to be exact. Mom and Dad were winging their way to New Orleans after almost missing the airport limo and blaming each other loudly. My parents always fight before they go away to be romantic. They'd handed me a list of house rules that were not to be broken under penalty of epic torture:

> No parties
> No boys (no problem there)
> No long-distance calls to Cousin Hannah
> in London
> No shopping sprees
> No late-night TV no matter who is on

Mom said that she absolutely trusted me and hoped I had a good time. Dad glared at my F2 like it was a tarantula and said they'd be calling *regularly*.

I was thinking about parental power and the rigors of unrequited love. I was doing this while standing in the Benjamin Franklin High Sports Stadium surrounded by shrieking teenage basketball fans who were reacting to every missed Piranha basket as a personal affront. My expert eyes searched the crowds for telling Valentine-cover moments.

It had been a killer game.

At halftime we'd been blistered 33 to 17 by the St. Ignatius Rams, who were, in my opinion, total sheep. Bobby Pershing, our center forward (we'd dated twice) had made a series of colossal dumb throws, causing Coach Gasser to turn purple, sputter, and bounce, which caused Bobby to miss a rebound and tip the ball perfectly through the other team's hoop as the Rams' coach, Father Bacardi, smiled his priest smile. Coach Gasser stormed off the court at halftime making veiled references to "indigent baboons," and I got several insult close-ups that captured the stark drama of amateur sports.

During halftime I tried to ignore Peter and Julia huddled on the far left bleacher. I tried to photograph him without her, which didn't work because she kept kissing his cheek. The Purple Piranhas Marching Band played "Finlandia," which made everyone feel stalwart except me. My heart ruptured as the Piranha cheerleaders leapt onto center court shrieking that artery-pumping Piranha cry:

> *Bite, bite, bite!*
> *Stick it in your ear!*
> *Aggressive fish*
> *Are the winners here!*

The cheer was picked up by the home fans and thundered through the stadium. I did deep breathing exercises to cope and hardly even cared when in the second half the Piranhas owned the court and battled their way to a stunning 42 to 42 tie in the final moments of play. That's when Bobby Pershing was fouled with malicious intent, and why he now stood at the free-throw line dripping with sweat, emotion carved into his profile. If he missed the throw we could lose the game, which meant the St. Ignatius Rams would win, and everyone hated them, even their nuns. Carl Yolanta hoisted me on his shoulders so I could get a close-up shot of Bobby's basketball (which better be perfectly aimed) sailing into the net, proving to the world that the Benjamin Franklin Piranhas were *back* from six weeks of degradation and defeat. Peter and Julia stood with the rest of the crowd, their arms around each other so you couldn't tell where one started and the other began. I checked the shutter speed on my F2 and told Carl to stop wiggling.

The whistle blew; the crowd went ballistic. I readied my flash as Bobby bounced, aimed. The ball left Bobby's hands. Up, up it went.

I waited, anticipating the peak moment of action. The ball cleared the rim.

I clicked just as it plopped into the hoop.

The home fans exploded. The visitors sagged. Peter and Julia hugged in ecstasy. Carl put me down gently and ran onto the court. I shouted "We're number one!" with everyone else, and leaned bleakly against a Coke machine.

"We're going, A.J." Trish Beckman placed a determined hand on my shoulder.

I knew what she meant and I didn't want to do it. "I'm going home, Trish."

She yanked me out of the stadium. "It's never too late to change your life!"

CHAPTER THREE

The Piranhas' losing streak had been deadly for business at the Pizza Pavilion, but now that we were back on top, Bo, the owner, was in fat city, doling out free sodas and advice ("Winners think like winners," "Losers think like losers"). I had allowed myself forty-five minutes of celebration time and then I was going home to develop my film and crumble into abject despair.

Trish patted my shoulder. "You're always complaining about not meeting any great guys. Well, A.J., here they are!"

I looked across the Pizza Pavilion but was not knocked out by male greatness. A group of senior boys was doing the Piranha Stomp, a dance performed with crazed arm-flapping motions while making loud hissing and glubbing noises.

"David Klein," Trish announced like a tour guide, "just broke up with that girl in New Leonard. He's available."

"He's making glubbing noises," I pointed out.

"How about Bill Peck?"

"He's wearing a hat with fins, Trish. He has a straw hanging out of his nostril."

Trish sighed. "Let's consider the basketball players —a key dating source, A.J., since you are almost five nine . . ."

I shook my head. I was in love with Peter Terris; she *knew* this. Every other male dripped mediocrity.

"There are lots of nice guys out there, A.J., who don't have chiseled jaws and who aren't going out with Death Incarnate. Let's not do the Todd Kovich number again!"

I set my jaw. Okay, so Todd and I had crashed and burned. It was inevitable. I was artsy. He was preppie. I cared too much. He didn't care at all. One of the many things wrong with Todd and me as a couple was that whenever we were together I wanted to be prettier, more popular, someone he would stay with. I knew all along he wouldn't stay.

Trish was moving in for her next big hit. "You are a wonderful person, A.J., an attractive person, and you fall for a guy's image without knowing the person behind it."

I said I hadn't asked to be born a perfectionist. I was just attracted to gorgeous.

"Are you going to slump around, A.J., waiting for another impossible guy?"

"Probably."

Trish bent over our veggie pizza and muffled a Drama Guild scream. She is going to be a psychologist and is always looking for someone to practice on. We'll be sitting at Duck's, our favorite junkie cheap food joint. I'll be about to bite into hot-dog heaven when Trish raps the prefab table with her plastic fork and says, "Now, A.J., about your wounded inner child . . ." I tell her that my inner child is swell, thanks, and would she please pass the mustard? Trish says I am an intriguing candidate for psychotherapy owing to my manifold resistance and intense denial system.

We became best friends at her eleventh birthday party when we got stuck at the top of a Ferris wheel together. Trish kept me from screaming—you could see the therapist in her even back then. She said to talk and not look down. We talked about never getting invited to Melissa Pageant's parties. We talked about who we had crushes on. We talked about how much we loved to ice skate and how someday we would star in the Ice Capades.

We still love to skate. Trish can twirl, but I'm faster. We skate on Pilling Pond early in the morning before the little kids take over, going round and round, surrounded by evergreens and holly, yakking away. Then Trish breaks off and goes into the center to twirl; I blast around the pond, feeling the miracle of ice and speed. When Robbie Oldsberg dumped me last February we went skating together and Trish didn't twirl once.

A squeal rose from the back of the Pizza Pavilion. Lisa Shooty, Head Cheerleader, was wiggling out of a booth, trying to get away from Al Costanzo, Star Running Back, who was waving a slice of pepperoni pizza at her full, sensuous mouth. All the popular students at the back tables roared, while the rest of us smiled thinly, wondering what was so funny, and why we so wanted to be in on it.

I studied the overflowing booths of popular students lining the back wall. There they were, the movers and shakers of Benjamin Franklin High—the sports stars, the cheerleaders, the good, the great, the gorgeous —bent over their pizzas.

Trish sensed my angst and said, "My mother says girls like Lisa Shooty get the ultimate curse known to man."

"What's that?"

"Too much too soon."

I looked at poor, cursed Lisa, who had been sprayed with sex appeal at birth. She had gleaming teeth and long, raven-black curls. She threw back her head and laughed with diamond-studded joy.

"When do you think the curse takes effect?" I asked.

"Not in our lifetime," Trish answered.

We contemplated this sickening truth as the cholesterol congealed on our Veggie Supremo. Then the front door of the Pizza Pavilion swung open and Peter Terris floated in like visiting royalty with Julia Hart epoxied to his side.

"Forget him!" Trish hissed.

They moved entwined to a window booth that magically emptied, moved right by me, I might add— I, who had just sold him an unusual pie hours before. Peter's surfer-sandy hair was shining, his ice-green eyes were gleaming. Julia shook her majestic blond hair and beamed at Peter like a politician's wife. I pushed my plate away.

"There's no way, A.J." Trish pushed the plate back toward me. "Some battles can't be won. Peter Terris is out of your universe and even if you got together, *which you won't,* he'd make you miserable because he's in love with himself just like Todd Kovich and Robbie Oldsberg and all the other guys you—"

"He has," I growled, "a healthy self-image!"

"He can't," Trish countered, "pass a mirror without checking his reflection!" She pointed to Peter, who had caught his perfect image in the window and was smoothing his hair. Trish held her hand up like a traffic cop. "You need to connect with a guy who's real, A.J., not these model types you get hung up on."

I rose to defend him, but was stopped short by Pearly Shoemaker, who was standing at our table smiling benevolently—a new approach. Her smile said if I handed over the Valentine's edition cover shot nobody would get hurt.

"I'm working on it, Pearly."

"I'm so glad, A.J." Her neck muscles gripped. "The entire Valentine's Day edition has been sold *without* a cover shot for advertisers!"

She slapped a poster trumpeting the Valentine *Oracle* with dumpy cupids flying in formation like Canada geese. I said cupids were mythological control freaks, *not* the symbol of a new generation.

Pearly closed her mascaraed eyes. "I'm counting to ten, A.J. I am the editor and my vision has prevailed, a vision that weaves classic love with today's relationships. *Everyone* likes cupids, A.J.!"

I made the universal barf sign in response.

Pearly turned to Trish. "Talk to her!"

Trish, loyal sidekick, wouldn't dream of it.

"I need the cover photo, A.J.!" Pearly hissed. *"You have thirty-six hours!"* She turned on her designer heel and stormed off.

"The shark woman strikes again," said Trish.

I looked at Julia. I looked at Peter. I hid my face in my hands.

Trish leaned forward. "There are seven days before the King of Hearts Dance, A.J.! Girls ask boys, *no* exceptions. And if you don't ask someone soon, you're going to end up sitting home *again,* being miserable and depressed *again.* You made me promise to bug you about this until you did something. So I'm bugging you!"

"I release you from your promise." I zippered my black bomber jacket. "Are you ever going to ask Tucker to the dance?"

Trish looked down, embarrassed. Tucker Crawford was her latest heartthrob, the brash, opinionated investigative reporter on the *Oracle* who had uncovered potential food-poisoning problems in the school cafeteria.

"I'm working on it," she said.

Nina Bloomfeld pulled up a chair at our table, looking bleak. She had just broken up with Eddie Royce, who had been cheating on her.

"How's it going?" I asked.

"As expected," Nina said glumly, "when you do the really mature thing."

I sighed deeply with her.

"We should all just ask someone," Trish declared. "It's better than sitting home!"

"Who," I half shouted, "made these rules about sitting home being so awful? I mean, if there's only one person you want to go with and that person doesn't want to go with you, do you have to dredge up a love-equivalent just for a stupid dance? Is this what we've sunk to as a free-thinking female society?"

"We shouldn't need dates to be fulfilled," Trish insisted. Then she lowered her voice ominously. "But if we don't hurry up, you guys, only the nerds will be left."

I was driving Trish home in my almost-classic sixteen-year-old Volvo, zooming down Mariah Avenue. I was beat. A sad love song played on the radio; the singer and I had the same problem: we didn't understand love. The rules were too obtuse.

You like somebody, but shouldn't show it.
You flirt, instead of being straight on.
You dump someone you've spent important,
    caring time with when someone better
    comes along.

I looked at Trish, who was half asleep. I turned left at the Nickleby Novelty Company as a cat knocked over a pile of cardboard boxes. I felt my nostrils clog with vile allergens because just seeing a cat affected me adversely. A box rolled precariously into the street; I slammed on the brakes.

Trish sat up with a start.

A small thing rolled out of the box. It did a kind of half somersault and landed spread eagle in front of my Volvo. "What was that?" Trish asked sleepily.

"I don't know . . ."

I kept the headlights on and began to get out of the car . . .

"Stay in the car, A.J. It's late and something's weird!"

I peered over the dashboard, turned on my brights.

"Maybe you killed it," Trish offered.

I got out, and walked to the front of the car, my heart racing. I took one look at the thing in the street.

"Please," I said, giggling.

Trish was huddled in the car, motioning me to come back. I knelt down to get a better look. My headlights shone a yellow glow across the figure.

"What is it?" Trish shouted.

I laughed out loud.

It was a dilapidated cupid doll as big as my hand with a battered bow-and-arrow and a stupid grin.

I picked it up.

He looked like the Pillsbury Doughboy dressed up for Valentine's Day. He had black painted eyes and a ripped mouth. He was naked except for a little pink sash that covered his lower extremities. I checked under the sash. He had Ken-doll anatomy.

Trish got out of the car and took one look at the cupid. "You've got to be kidding," she scoffed.

I brushed the doll off, giggling. He was plump, squishy, and *totally* Coney Island. His cheek had a rip in it, stuffing oozed out.

"I think," I said throwing the cupid in the air, "I have my cover shot."

Trish stepped back. "Pearly will hang you in the Student Center, A.J., if you—"

"She wanted cupids, Trish."

Trish stared at the doll blankly. "You've lost it, A.J."

"It's got personality," I said, heading for the car.

"It's got fleas!"

We got in the car. I buckled the seat belt around the doll in the backseat because the true bonding between photographer and still-life object cannot begin until the photographer sees life in the nonliving. I parted its dinky head and opened myself to the relationship.

"I am Allison Jean McCreary," I declared, "master still-life photographer. You have only thirty-six hours to show me who you are!"

I threw the cupid into my studio and crashed down the garage steps, needing sleep. Tomorrow I would take the cover shot.

I stumbled to the upstairs bathroom with Stieglitz at my heels and told my artistic brain to think about something other than the fact that the old pipes in our old house were creaking and groaning like a maniac murderer was trying to break in. Our house was over a hundred years old and came with a century of problems that helped you forget its rambling charm. I locked the bathroom door and shoved a small vanity in front of it.

There was a crash and a flurry as Stieglitz jumped on the toilet seat. He leapt down, pawed the carpet, and turned in quick, choppy moves.

"Easy, boy!"

Stieglitz shuddered, yelped. I told him to *sit*. He didn't. Stieglitz only sat at dog-obedience school with master canine trainer Steve Bloodworth, who resembled a pit bull on a bad day. I unlocked the door, shoved the vanity aside, and let Stieglitz leave to patrol the hall.

I plodded to my bedroom. Stieglitz was shaking by the window in uncurbed neurosis. I stepped across the heap of dirty clothes that had missed my hamper and climbed into my futon as Stieglitz whined pathetically at my feet.

I pulled my fat flannel quilt up to my chin and waited for sleep.

I counted sheep.

I counted gorgeous guys.

I counted Stieglitz's barks that were about to shatter glass.

Stieglitz pounced on me. *"What?"* I jumped out

of bed. He was running in circles, pawing at the door.

"What is it?" Stieglitz looked at me through dark, hunted eyes. *"All right"*—I yanked on my L. L. Bean arctic slipper socks—*"show me!"*

CHAPTER FOUR

Stieglitz tore down the hall thrashing his tail and screeched to a halt at the foot of my studio steps, yelping like mad. I raced after him as the clock struck midnight (only figuratively—it was digital). Stieglitz shot up the stairs and rammed his head against my studio door with the sign on it that read DON'T EVEN THINK ABOUT ENTERING.

A weirdness wound its way like smoke into the night. It was creepy, crawly. The wind picked up outside. Stieglitz howled like a wolf in the wilderness.

"What is it, boy?"

Stieglitz scratched at the door in a fury, taking off paint, trying to shove it open.

"Everything," I screamed, *"is all right!"*

My hand clutched the doorknob. I took a massive breath, pushed the door open . . .

Stieglitz bolted through it and stopped barking.

I leaned against the doorway and froze.

The cupid!

He was standing there looking at me with fiery black eyes and little rosy cheeks, standing there *breathing*!

The cupid shook his legs and arms like an aerobics instructor.

He fluttered his clear, thin wings.

He rolled his head back and forth and did a couple of quick karate chops on his muscled legs.

I looked madly around to see if I was dreaming . . .

The cupid put his minuscule hands on his equally teeny waist and peered at me.

I clutched my throat and sank to my knees.

"Are you"—I gasped—"are you . . . *real?*"

A slight smile flickered across his face. He lifted two feet in the air, spun like a twirling top, and landed on my still-life pedestal.

I started hyperventilating.

"Are you . . ." I struggled for words. *"What* are you?"

He cleared his throat. "Well, now," he said in a full-sized voice, "shall we begin?"

"*You talk!*"

"I do many things." He brushed off his dinky bow-and-arrow.

Moments passed.

Years, maybe.

The cupid scooped a teeny red apple from his satchel and took a bite.

I stared at him, awestruck. It was like a million Disney movies rolled into one. I grinned and hugged my knees with delight. I felt five years old.

I could make him a little bed out of a shoebox.

I could sew him eensy-weensy clothes and he could go everywhere with me in my pocket!

I was dying to touch him. I held out my hand. "Come on," I cooed, "I won't hurt you."

The cupid rose indignantly to his full height, which wasn't much. "I am," he informed me, "a master archer! *Not* a plaything!"

I yanked my hand back. "I'm . . . sorry . . . I . . ."

He stared at me defiantly. I looked away. The cupid could be an extraterrestrial!

He marched up to me and stamped his foot. "I am not," he insisted, "an extraterrestrial!"

"Did I say that?" I croaked.

"You were thinking it."

"How do you know what I was thinking?"

The cupid beamed.

"What planet are you from?"

He shook his head in disbelief. "You must rid your mind of the dowdy American notion that anything you don't understand comes from outer space."

We stared at each other. I grabbed a pair of scissors from a table. *"What kind of trick is this?"*

"I do not perform tricks." He zoomed off the pedestal and lighted on the rug. "But I do have many talents."

"Name one . . ."

The cupid pulled back the string of his bow and aimed his arrow at the Granny Smith apple on my still-life pedestal. He concentrated on his target as his left hand rested at eye level and his right hand, which drew the string, bent above his right shoulder. It shot across the room, hit the apple dead center, and reverberated with a little sound:

Thwonk.

A satisfied grin swept across his face; he remained in shoot position for a moment, then he flew to retrieve the arrow, which he put in a leather satchel behind his back.

"I consult," he said. "Free of charge. This"—he patted the leather case—"is not a satchel, it is a quiver."

"Did I say that?"

He looked at me. I had thought it. I pulled at my nightgown and shivered.

"There is nothing," he assured me, "to fear."

Right.

"I am here merely to assist you," he continued. "No strings attached." He floated to the ceiling and hovered there.

I swallowed hard. "What's the catch?"

"There is no catch."

"There's always a catch."

"No catch," he insisted. He was giving my studio a good once-over. "Our relationship can only succeed if we build a relationship of trust."

"You want me to trust you?"

He began to sharpen his arrow furiously like he was chalking a pool cue. "Teenage consultations are endlessly troublesome!"

"What do you know about teenagers?"

Sadness flickered in his eyes. "I know a great deal about *you*," he said finally. "It is my job to know." The cupid swooped down to my gallery of framed prints. "Your work is very moody. Technically, it is excellent, but if you concentrated on more positive aspects of life, you would see an energy coming from your art."

"There's energy all over my art!"

"Negative energy," he said with conviction. "It is a powerful force, but not as strong as positive expression." He flew over to my east wall and gave my framed prints a once-over. He hovered at my picture of a melting snowman at dusk that spoke volumes about relationships.

"I would experiment more with early-morning light if I were you," he said.

I stepped back. "I know all about light."

Stieglitz found his nerve and approached the cupid like he was checking out a squirrel he might want to chase. The cupid, unafraid, stretched out his little hand.

"Sit," said the cupid. Stieglitz sat. "Good dog," said the cupid, rearranging his sash. "You should brush him more," he continued. "The keeshond breed needs constant attention."

"I brush him all the time!"

The cupid looked right through me. "Lying erodes the fabric of all relationships."

"We don't have a relationship!"

"We could"—the cupid leaned on my purple Persian floor-pillow—"if you let your defenses down. It's up to you."

I ran out of my studio and down two flights of stairs. I had spent years building up my defenses and I liked them just fine. I yanked the phone off the jack and dialed zero.

"Operator," said a terse female voice.

"Is this Connecticut?" I demanded. *"Have we all shifted into another dimension?"*

I heard a click.

"Operator?"

I sat in the chair holding the receiver in my hand. I

held it so long that the buzzing noise started. A computer voice said I had to hang up. I gripped it.

The air hung still and weird. My ears strained for the sound of good old reality. A car drove by blaring rock music and threw a beer can onto the driveway.

I was still in Connecticut.

I stood on the safe side of my studio door with Stieglitz. All was quiet but I wasn't fooled. I snapped my fingers and Stieglitz leapt to attention. "I give you permission, Stieglitz, to do whatever is required. Maiming, destroying, terrorizing. You're in charge."

Stieglitz yelped and crashed down the stairs. I glared at him. I was aching to peer inside my studio.

Was the cupid still there?

My studio door opened, the cupid fluttered out, and announced, "Come in, for heaven's sake, we don't have much time!"

The cupid flew straight up, then darted in a zigzag. He hovered by the banister, flew backward, and plopped on my shoulder. My throat closed. My palms went gummy.

"Who," I whimpered, "are you?"

"Ah, now, that is an excellent question." He did an aerial loop off my shoulder.

I looked at him as much as I dared. "I need to know what's going on!"

He hovered by my studio window and gazed at the stars. "What is going on depends upon you," he said. "You're in control, Allison Jean McCreary, of what you choose to examine in your life."

I gripped the doorknob.

The cupid's face darkened. "I've always wondered why people are so afraid to trust."

I clutched my heart.

Sadness flashed in his eyes again. "Some things in life can only be learned through trust." He fingered his bow slowly.

A wave of warmth was oozing over me, drawing me to something I didn't understand.

"You must listen to the things that you try to ignore," he commanded.

The cupid zipped to the window and fluttered his wings. "I see you're frowning, my friend. For a while I expect you to be most miserable."

The cupid hovered over my right knee like Tinkerbell with an attitude. I sat on my shaking hands.

He raised his teeny bow. "There is no time to dawdle!"

I watched him, dumbstruck. Then suddenly, magically, I saw the answer to one of my problems. I was inches away from the photograph of the century! I'd call *Life, National Geographic,* the London *Times, People,* and

Scientific American. I would become famous. I picked up my F2 behind my back and smiled.

The cupid shook his head. "Only you can see me, my friend. I am not photographable."

I held my camera tight. "Let's just make sure . . ." I raised the camera to eye level, my keen eye instantly catching the essence of a bona fide, flitting miracle . . . my finger whooshed across the clicker, which was . . .

Stuck.

Blast!

I slammed the clicker down again. It was no use.

"This," said the cupid, "is an excellent time to inform you of the laws governing the Visitation." He did an aerial somersault and landed on my bookcase. "First and foremost, only *you* can see me"—he smiled at Stieglitz—"and your dog, of course." Stieglitz barked at the word *dog* and looked confused. "Secondly, you are to tell no one of the Visitation, until such time as you have reached a deeper plane of understanding and can address the experience with maturity and clarity.

"Thirdly," the cupid explained, "we must press on or the Visitation will be rendered incomplete; we have a short period in which to accomplish monumental tasks, which will become clear to you in the doing—not until then. And fourthly"—the cupid hovered to the right of my nose—"I have come to assist you, Allison Jean Mc-

Creary, not to harm you. The sooner you believe this basic tenet, the quicker we can proceed."

I gulped. Earth rules I could handle:

Smile at someone and they'll smile at you.
Take the lens cap off the camera before you
    take the picture.
Never date a hockey player.

But when you're dealing with the cosmos, all bets are off.

The cupid rapped his quiver. "You have a photography deadline, I believe? A deadline that has brought you discouragement?"

I looked away. He had that right.

"It is possible," the cupid said, "to reverse discouragement."

I positioned myself on my purple Persian pillow with guarded body language.

"You were trying to please others with this photography assignment on love," the cupid said, "not yourself."

That frosted me! *He* hadn't been battling massive unrequitedness. *He* didn't have Pearly Shoemaker as a gut-busting editor.

"You cannot blame others, my friend. You are discouraged because you have not been true to your vision."

"I don't have a vision for love right now! That's my problem! Would you please stop reading my mind?"

"I'm afraid that is impossible. It is not within my power to disconnect us. Confusion, when addressed, can bring forth clarity. Find something that reflects how you feel about love and photograph it."

"Thanks for that little tip! What do you think I've been doing for the last two months—skiing in Aspen? I've got massive blisters from trudging around this town trying to find one lousy shot that commemorates teenage love!"

I stamped my foot, because I'd started to cry. *"I'm sorry!"* I wailed.

I buried my head as the cupid sighed impatiently. How was I supposed to express myself as an artist when every time I tried to photograph something about teenage love, I heard this little voice say that I would love Peter Terris until the day I died and he would never even notice me?

I was crying like a complete dolt, curled up in the fetal position on my purple Persian floor-pillow. The cupid glided over and handed me a tissue. "Blow," he directed. "You need not fear this photography assignment. Art that reflects the heart and soul will always communicate with others." He fluttered to the studio door. "You will sleep now, my friend."

My heart thumped wildly. "I don't understand what's happening!"

"We can only hope that you will learn before it is too late," the cupid responded solemnly. "We have been put together for a reason, Allison Jean McCreary. You need what I can teach you, and I"—he looked away sadly—"must right a wrong."

My sinuses throbbed.

"My last Teenage Visitation was not deemed successful," he continued. "When a cupid errs, he must right the wrong or he will never find peace."

I bolted up. "You *erred*?"

"It was a combination of my failing and the young lady's, I assure you."

"You're not good at this?"

"I much prefer visiting persons in their golden years, persons who have a wealth of life experience from which to—"

"I got a second-string cupid?"

He shot straight up, engulfed by fury. *"You will sleep!"*

He fluttered his dinky wings.

My feet started moving against my will; I stumbled downstairs to my bedroom with Stieglitz at my side. I shouted that no one could sleep with this amount of compacted stress in their lives; the teenage mind was not meant to carry such trauma!

I flopped my head on my pillow and crashed into dreamland; don't ask me why.

CHAPTER FIVE

I woke up at 6:33 A.M., not on my own. The cupid opened my blinds and announced, "Get up, my friend. There is much to accomplish." He zoomed to the foot of my futon and perched there like a bird.

"What. . . ," I stammered, "needs accomplishing?"

He fluttered his wings, and pulled off my plaid quilt. "Get up," he ordered. "I can only assist you if you get out of bed."

I shivered. "What happened with you and that other teenager?"

The cupid glowed with irritation. "It is a personal issue that does not concern you."

"Everything about you concerns me."

"We will not speak of this again!" The cupid blew sky high like a puny cannonball. "Wash, please!" He pushed me toward the bathroom and pulled the door open.

I stood fast. "I want to know who you are, where you come from, and what's going on on!"

"*Silence!*" The cupid fluttered his tiny wings in irritation.

I turned on the faucet and started washing my face like a machine that had been plugged in.

"For some," the cupid acknowledged, "trusting is a long journey."

I washed my face longer than usual, hoping that Neutrogena and water would bring clarity; they didn't. The cupid handed me a face towel like a butler. "Please be dressed in ten minutes."

I clutched the towel.

"And bring your camera."

He fluttered his wings, closed *my* bathroom door, and left me in the blackness of the final frontier.

It was 7:13, Sunday morning. Stieglitz, the cupid, and I moved down the sun-soaked, frozen streets of Crestport, Connecticut, just as normal as you please. We turned by the police station and its somber, crime-busting hedges.

The cupid did a triple back loop and dive-bombed a patrol car. I clung to a lamppost.

Help! I wanted to shout.

"Turn right, please," said the cupid.

"Where are you taking me?"

"To the beach."

"Why?"

"Patience, my friend. You must learn to see with new eyes."

I grumbled that if seeing with new eyes meant losing touch with gravity, I was against it. I crabbed that it was unnerving to take orders from a creature that only I could see! I pointed a shaking finger at the cupid and felt a tap on my shoulder.

I swung around to face a very large policeman.

"Everything okay, miss?"

"Uh . . ."

He put his hand on his nightstick. "You want to talk about it, miss?"

The cupid zipped around the officer's head and landed on his hat. My mind stretched toward its outer limits. I said I had the lead in the school play and that I was acting out my part, which took place on a bleak, wintry street so that I could sense the cold, numbing futility of my character in her true surroundings. I took a huge breath and prayed.

"Well, now," said the officer, "that sounds like some play, little lady."

I said believe me, it was the role of a lifetime, and

backed away onto Browning Road looking massively dramatic. Trish would have been proud. Stieglitz strained on the leash, his tail dragging.

"Heel," the cupid commanded him.

Stieglitz clipped into a perfect heel. Traitor. The cupid zipped along millimeters from my earlobe.

I shuddered. "I almost got arrested for being a psycho!"

The cupid soared upward and swooped down; his wings buzzed faintly. "Turn left, please."

"It's prettier over here—"

"*Left!*" he ordered.

I went left past the huge stone houses set back from the Crestport Beach.

"A little past these bushes," he directed. "Let your dog off the leash and open yourself to the experience."

I groaned that I'd had enough experiences for one day and released Stieglitz to careen on the snowy sand. The cupid motioned me forward. He soared over the boarded-up Snack Shack. He perched on the lifeguard's chair. He skimmed the polluted water of Long Island Sound as it splashed against the rocks and went back again in nothing resembling waves.

"How do you do that?" I whispered.

The cupid zoomed through the air as the wind whooshed across the sloppy gray lot.

I kept walking. I loved the beach in winter. It was wild and free without that putrid smell of suntan lotion.

I didn't even mind February because I was partial to black-and-white photography. All that silvery beauty and subtle tonality.

I pulled up my collar and shoved my hands in my pockets as it started to snow. I lifted my face as the big flakes fell. They glided from heaven and covered the beach.

A Heinz ketchup bottle washed up on shore and I remembered sitting on this very beach with Todd Kovich who said I was rare and pretty and who kissed me like he meant it. Two hours later he went to Yale.

I jammed the Heinz ketchup bottle between two rocks and tore off five quick shots. It spoke to me. About rich people in big boats who dump their trash without paying the price. About massive oil spills and disappearing rain forests. About mounting nuclear waste and Julia Hart.

That's when I saw it.

Just to the left of the embankment that jutted out to the Sound. It was painted on a huge, craggy rock set apart from the rest. It read:

DONNA LOVES ~~STEVE~~
~~GARY~~
~~DEREK~~
~~NATHANIEL~~
DONNA IS CONFUSED

I laughed as snow twinkled down. Love in the age of angst! It was perfect Valentine funk.

"Of course it's perfect," the cupid said hovering over the rock.

"How did you know about this? I was here five days ago; I didn't see it."

A sunbeam illuminated the scene. "Make available light work for you, my friend."

"Yes. I know what to do."

I focused my F2 to the left of the rock. I studied the rock, looking for the best angle—from the right, I decided. The sun soaked into Donna's muddle, the rock sparkled like quartz. I tore off four shots that would immortalize Donna in the hearts and minds of millions of Americans. I worked quickly, not knowing how long the sunbeam effect would last. I remembered my father's words: "Let the camera know what you're feeling."

I took a deep breath. I was feeling strangely in control. I moved in close (amateurs forget this), caught the rock in stark detail at an angle that made it look like a gravestone, and blurred the surrounding elements by going to a wide aperture setting. A pigeon landed on the rock.

"Perfect," I whispered, "keep it steady, steady . . ."

The pigeon posed standing, pecking. I watched for small moments when he would reveal himself. He squawked. I caught it. He scratched. I got that too.

"Fly," I told him.

He fluttered like a butterfly and I jiggled the camera on purpose to get an impressionistic blur that would no doubt get me a four-year photography scholarship at NYU. I was perspiring despite the cold and focused in close for the Ultimate Rock Shot, capturing the consummate confusion of my generation. My finger lowered the shutter, light streaked against the film.

"You've got it," the cupid said, fluttering down.

"I want another roll." I plopped new film into the camera.

He shook his head. "Another roll is not necessary."

"I'm the photographer," I reminded him. "You're—"

"Jonathan," the cupid said, extending his hand.

I took it gently. It was the size of a fingernail, weird and marvelous. "Jonathan," I said softly.

Suddenly the sunbeam brilliance disappeared; clouds covered the sky. Without that light we had nothing. You can't trust a natural phenomenon.

"There is very little time, my friend!" The cupid whistled to Stieglitz, who bounded over. "We must press on!"

I unzipped my jacket. The cupid fluttered his wings impatiently.

"What kind of cupid are you?" I whispered.

Jonathan smiled and motioned me toward home.

Jonathan was zooming around my darkroom like a euphoric bee while I was in the critical stage of developing high-contrast film, when the image must be brought out without losing the detail. This stage made the difference between a nice photograph you put in an album and one that sold for cold cash. I was agitating the film-developer tank assertively like I always do for the first thirty seconds, I was then going to agitate it in twenty-second intervals, going a full four minutes to bring out the light, when Jonathan said I would lose the textures if I agitated that long. That's when I said that I could do this in my sleep, thank you, *I* didn't need advice from a dinky Ansel Adams. Jonathan fluttered his wings, which caused me to lose count, which left me no choice except to fix and rinse the film early rather than risk overdevelopment. The prints were stellar: the early light beamed across the DONNA IS CONFUSED like a laser.

"You're welcome," said Jonathan.

"All right," I sighed, "I was wrong." I hung the wet shot on my clothesline to dry and sat back, supremely satisfied. "They're great, Jonathan. Thank you."

Jonathan took out his arrow, fixed it expertly in his bow . . .

"What do you do with that thing?" I asked.

Jonathan pulled his muscled right arm back, pulled the string tighter, tighter; his eyes squinted at the minuscule root-beer stain on my wall, hardly visible through the glow of my red safelight. He concentrated on his target, pulled the arrow back to cheek level, never losing control. He let the arrow fly; it shot through the air sure and true and landed dead center in the small brown blob.

Thwonk.

Jonathan stayed in shoot position until his breathing returned to normal.

"I bring truth," he said quietly, and flew to retrieve the arrow.

I pulled the Volvo into Pearly's steep driveway. Her two-story front window was framed with cupid posters proclaiming, IT'S COMING SOON. I got out of the Volvo and smirked. "I've got news for you, Pearly. *It's here!*"

Jonathan glared at the cupid posters in Pearly's window. "Positively boorish!" he declared.

Pearly's house was a flashy, modern concoction of steel and glass that was the bane of the Crestport Beautification Council, which had declared it "anti–New England." I trudged up the walkway that was bordered with jutting rocks. Jonathan flew alongside me; I was getting used to this, and it concerned me. I rang the doorbell and waited.

Pearly answered the door in an electric-pink jumpsuit with matching glasses. "Is this good news or bad news?" she asked.

I dangled four DONNA IS CONFUSED enlargements in her face. Great art needs no introduction.

Pearly's face turned to sunshine.

Not massive sunshine, because getting Pearly to beam was like waking the dead. "Ooooohhhhh," she said excitedly, looking at the prints. "It's weird, but it's—it's . . . *totally today!* I take back everything I've ever said about you, A.J.—everything I was thinking even, which, believe me, was much worse."

"I can only imagine."

"It's not traditional; it's not lacy; it's not . . ."

"Trite?" I suggested. "Overdone?"

"Let's not kill the moment, A.J."

"Pearly, have I ever let you down before?"

"Once," she said, frowning at the memory.

She was referring to the fiasco over my *Oracle* Christmas cover of Mr. Kendrake, the senior-class advisor, dressed in a Santa suit and smoking a Camel in the teachers' lounge. Dr. Strictland, the principal, had split a kidney when she saw it and lambasted the *Oracle* staff about sensitivity versus journalistic fervor as one of the iridescent fish in the aquarium behind her desk went belly up like an omen of things to come.

"That cover captured the anxiety of public-school teachers in America!" I protested. "It became an *underground classic*!"

"It *became*," she hissed, "my personal nightmare."

She held the prints to the light as Jonathan fluttered in, perched on the steel staircase, and waved. Pearly put her hand on my shoulder. "Who is Donna?"

"A tortured soul, Pearly. I like to think that in some small way we all know Donna."

She nodded. "What do you think about putting a cute little cupid in the corner?"

Jonathan brightened.

"Spare me, Pearly."

"A Nude Dude." She giggled, her face awash in headlines. "What rhymes with *dude*, A.J.?"

"*Crude*, Pearly. *Lewd*."

Jonathan fluttered his wings. *"Really!"*

She shook her curls. "I'm knocked out by this, A.J.; besieged! It stands on its own. Forget the cupid."

Pearly stood in front of a large modern painting that resembled a pencil. "Maybe we should print three thousand copies. With this cover and my vision we can take America by storm!" Pearly ran to get a folder. "The Valentine issue is a hit, A.J.! Advertisers have embraced my vision!" She waved an ad in my face. "Haggermeyer's Funeral Home Salutes Love and the Teenage Years. Does that get you or what?"

"It gets me, Pearly."

"Here's a coupon from Jocko's Towing."

"What to give the Valentine who has everything . . ."

"And Sudderman's Jiffy Lube took out a *full page ad,* A.J., to announce their frequent-luber discount plan. I've got articles coming on Blind Dates, Cheap Restaurants, What's In/What's Out, How to Tell If You're *Really* in Love, and"—she lowered her voice for impact —"Embarrassing Dating Moments!"

I could write that one. "We have to go, Pearly."

"We do?" Pearly looked confused.

"Careful," warned Jonathan.

"I mean, *I* have to go. I, singular, one entity . . ."

Jonathan flew through the closed door, a pretty decent trick, considering. Pearly's Siamese slinked down the stairs and rubbed against me; my sinuses clogged. Jonathan zipped back inside and asked if I was coming.

"I'm coming," I said.

Pearly's face froze.

"I mean I'm going . . ."

I sneezed.

"Say good-bye," said Jonathan.

I said it and tore down her front steps with Jonathan zigging and zagging.

"We can now proceed to the next level of the Visitation," Jonathan informed me. "A level that is fraught with complications."

"I'll pass, thanks."

"Passing," said Jonathan, plucking the string on his little bow, "is not an option."

CHAPTER SIX

Jonathan perched on the ceiling fan, pouting. I had asked about the Other Teenager again, just in passing. He said, "The subject is closed."

I was slumped on the kitchen couch, wondering if I had the strength to make it upstairs. The phone rang; I reached for it shakily.

"Hello. . . ," I croaked.

"A.J.! Are you all right?"

It was my mother sounding Very Worried. Smart woman. "We've left a few messages, honey."

I looked at the answering machine that was blinking madly and opted for the pithy teenage avoidance version. "I was out, Mom."

Mom paused, her keen parental antenna picking up latent child stress. "You sound strained," she offered.

I nodded; I was strained.

"You sound . . . exhausted . . ."

I nodded again; she was two for two. "Are you guys having fun?" I asked, hoping someone was.

"The food is not to be believed. The weather is gorgeous. We've gained five pounds in twelve hours. We slept until nine!" She paused, "A.J., is everything okay?"

"Things are—"

"Careful," warned Jonathan, peeking down from the ceiling fan.

"Wide open at this point, Mother."

"A.J., you don't sound like yourself."

Tell me about it. Jonathan fluttered his wings toward the phone; I closed my eyes and said everything was perfectly fine, a barefaced whopper. My mother sounded immensely relieved.

"Take care, sweetie," Mom said. "Dad sends his love."

My eyelids crashed shut. I curled into the fetal position. A certain winged being landed on my knee and tapped it with his quiver.

"What?" I cried.

"I want you," Jonathan directed, "to think about your three choices before answering. Once you decide, we cannot go back."

"What choices?"

"My short time with you," he explained firmly, fingering his arrow, "is to provide on-the-job training. I can help you with your professional life as an artist. You have already seen my keen artistic sense there. I can assist you academically." He raised his whisper-thin eyebrows. "Given your last report card, my friend, this could be terribly useful."

I cleared my throat. I'd gone from an A to a C in English Lit—Miss Bright had leveled my term paper because I had called Elizabeth Barrett Browning a "hopeless romantic who didn't know the first thing about modern relationships."

I leaned forward. "Let me get this straight. You're telling me you can make me a better photographer or a better student?"

"Precisely."

I grinned as that sank in.

"What's the third choice?"

"That, my dear, is not for you at this time."

"You said there were three choices!"

"I am duty bound to report that, yes, but such assistance is not appropriate for—"

"Tell me the third choice!"

He spun around like a thing on fire. "I can also

assist you romantically, but I would vehemently advise against that!"

I leapt up. *"Romantically how?"*

Jonathan ricocheted off the wall. "It is my professional opinion that romantic assistance would not be beneficial to you at this point!"

"Do you mean . . . that you shoot one of those things at somebody, somebody I choose, and they . . ."

"Succumb," Jonathan whispered.

I was thunderstruck. *"Succumb to, like, being in love with me?"*

"Unfortunately," he said, "but I must tell you that history has shown that manipulated relationships are never satisfying for long."

I pictured a golden arrow whizzing through space, ripping into Peter Terris's heart with an eensy, weensy *thwonk.*

Fire shot through me. "Is this my decision?"

He lowered his head. "Appallingly, yes."

"You do what I say?"

He nodded glumly. "But let me point out that I come with a breadth of experience and not to consult me would be highly—!"

"I know what I want!"

I leaned forward, my heart ablaze. "I want you to shoot Peter Terris with one of your arrows, Jonathan! I want you to get him for me!"

Jonathan flopped down, dejected. "I am not adept at Teenage Visitations!"

"You and I are going to drive to Peter's house," I shouted with ecstasy. "You are going to zap him with a poisoned arrow and I'm going to live happily ever after!"

Love, he ranted, isn't all it's drummed up to be, *especially* if we don't know the other person well at all, *especially* if we're crazy about a person just because of how they look! I assured him that how Peter looked was only a minuscule part of why I was mad about him.

He eyed me wearily. "Infatuation cannot be sustained indefinitely, my friend. Love that embraces the entire person is a monumental gift that takes time to grow!"

"*I don't have time to grow! The King of Hearts Dance is six days away, and I'm going! I'm going with Peter Terris because you're going to shoot him, Jonathan!*"

I grabbed my car keys, flung on my black bomber jacket, and headed to my Volvo and destiny.

Peter's Dutch Colonial was at the end of the Sweetwater Lane cul-de-sac; I drove up to it slowly, my heart thumping in my larynx. The Sunday *Times* was still in the driveway. The windows sparkled with promise and eternity. Peter's mother walked past the big bay window in a red robe, scratching her head and yawning. I smiled. Soon we would spend holidays together. I would be a model daughter-in-law: caring, hospitable, impervious to stinging criticism. I would keep my judgmental thoughts to myself, especially about the stupid stone pig statue on the front lawn that made a perfectly fine house look like an indoor petting zoo. Peter's mother glared out the window at the *Times* at the far end of the driveway and made an unsavory gesture in honor of the paper person. Maybe Jonathan should sprinkle her with something. I opened the car door to get out; Jonathan held up his hand.

"Stay here," he said quietly. "You cannot be present at the shooting."

He fluttered out of the car.

"This will be the last opportunity, my friend, for you to change your mind. Once the arrow pierces his heart, there is no turning back!"

"Pierce it, Jonathan!"

He whooshed out the door past a nervous woman walking a toy poodle. Love was in the air. I breathed it in deep as the poodle peed on my car. Jonathan flew past the stone pig statue and approached the green front door. He disappeared through it without a trace. I put on my sunglasses, slumped down, and waited with the engine running like the driver in a bank heist.

My ears strained, listening for the *thwonk.* I might not hear it, of course, since Jonathan's *thwonk*s were quiet—not surprising, given his size.

The sun hit my car windshield like a beacon. I sensed the eyes of every neighbor upon me. I looked suspicious. I drove around and around the cul-de-sac, waiting for Jonathan to appear. My sinuses filled; I blew my nose and told myself there were lots of reasons to be calm.

I checked my watch. Twenty-two minutes had passed and still no cupid. Something awful had happened!

A rush of guilt poured over me. Manipulating someone was an awful thing to do. I was a terrible person and now I was being punished!

I tore off my sunglasses. *I'm sorry,* I wailed inside.

Suddenly, like an angry bird, Jonathan shot out the Terrises' upstairs window and dived into my front seat.

"Go!" he shouted, breathing hard.

I rammed the Volvo into drive and took off. *"What happened? Did you do it?"*

"He kept moving," Jonathan said. "I am not certain that I got him."

I ripped the car to a stop.

"He was very resistant."

"You introduced yourself?"

"Of course not! His heart is hard!"

"What does that mean?"

"It means that we wait."

"How long do we wait?"

He looked at me with piercing eyes. "That depends upon the dimension of resistance."

I attempted to collect myself. "But if it didn't take, you go back, right?"

He was silent.

"You shoot him again, right?"

Jonathan looked sadly out the car window and said nothing.

CHAPTER SEVEN

It was Monday morning, 6 A.M. I'd hardly slept. Jonathan was watching me from the top shelf of my bookcase, leaning against my copy of *Alice in Wonderland,* which seemed bleakly symbolic.

"Don't you sleep?" I asked.

"Not during a Visitation. Get dressed, please. There is much to accomplish."

"Don't you have any idea what's going to happen?" I wailed.

Jonathan zoomed off the bookcase and fluttered

in my face. "It is too soon to determine the out-come."

"I could die from stress!"

Jonathan gave me a sympathetic pat and pirouet-ted on my shoulder.

"Patience, my friend."

I got dressed in my ice-green pants and floppy turtleneck that cleverly matched Peter's eyes, which would come in handy if he were to succumb today. My eyes looked puffy from severe sleep deprivation, my skin was a wan, pasty shade. I pulled on my black boots and tossed out my hair.

Mom had taught me the importance of an interest-ing, healthy breakfast. I went downstairs and ate a lemon nonfat yogurt without refined sugar, a happy, red McIntosh apple, and an Eskimo Pie. Jonathan hovered impatiently at the door, tapping his quiver.

"Shall we?" he asked, and did his through-the-door flitting trick. I tried to beam through the door too.

"Hey!" I bonged my nose on it, still earthbound.

Jonathan fluttered back through the door. *"I am the cupid,"* he directed. *"You are the . . ."* He groped here for proper terminology.

"Art professional," I whimpered.

We were off.

Benjamin Franklin High was awash in Valentine's Day magic. The King of Hearts Dance Committee had plastered red hearts everywhere; they twinkled from walls and ceilings. I stood by Peter Terris's locker, my arteries pumped in expectation. I touched it. This, ladies and gentlemen, could be the site where Peter Terris falls madly in love with A. J. McCreary, crashing at her feet in passion for all the world to see. Trish came by and accosted me.

"You look like cold oatmeal, A.J."

"Thank you, Trish."

"What happened?"

I shrugged.

She eyed me. "Something's going on."

"This and that."

"Start with *this,* A.J."

I smiled wearily.

"You're going out with someone."

"Noooooo . . ."

"You're planning something."

"Ummmmmm . . ."

"Tell me!"

It was killing me not to!

"Later," I said gently, and pushed through the crowded hall to Peter Terris, who had just filled the corridor with full-orbed gorgeousness.

"Hi," I said, searching his flawless face. He looked at me, half smiled, and walked away. I clutched my heart. Jonathan was zigzagging between comatose students. I motioned him into the bathroom. We went into a stall; I locked the door.

"I think he needs another arrow, Jonathan."

Jonathan sat on the toilet-paper roll and crossed his legs. "That is not the solution yet, my friend. These things take time."

I clenched my trembling hands. "Can't you speed things up? This is massive pressure!"

There was a knock on the stall door. *"A.J.?"*

I looked down to see a pair of familiar scuffed boots. I opened the stall door to Trish Beckman's psychiatric stare.

She reached out her hand. "A.J., senior year is a time of conflict. The old gang will soon be gone. No one really knows what college will bring. These are fears that grip us all. If you're trying to work out your feelings of abandonment by talking to yourself, you know I'm always here to listen."

"Thank you, Trish."

The fifth-period bell tolled. I ran to Art History class, slid into my desk near O'Keefe, Mr. Zeid's cactus, and tried to make sense of my crumbling life.

Mr. Zeid was wrestling with his slide projector from hell, trying to get it to focus and muttering about it being "the wretched refuse of an impoverished educational budget." He took a sip from his Botticelli coffee mug and told Carl Yolanta to turn out the lights. Carl grinned at me and put his hands together like he was praying.

I bolted up.

I'd forgotten about *the test*!

Mr. Zeid had warned us about it last week—"all encompassing" was how he'd described it—the educational euphemism for a Real Beast. I hadn't cracked a book because of Jonathan. My grade average would plummet.

Mr. Zeid passed out the test to quiet groans and wails. "Part one," he announced. "In twenty-five words or less, tell me the artist, what you think he was trying to say, and the greatest strength of the painting."

He kicked the slide projector from hell and the screen exploded with a Raphael fresco of four cupids circling a nymph, arrows drawn, ready to nail her into oblivion. I knew this one cold. I wrote that sometimes true love needs assistance and that the painting's strength was in numbers, specifically, the multiple ambushing cupids, providing critical backup in case the lead one missed. I moved to the question sheets and was hurled into space: "What was the precept of art according to Pope Gregory the Great?"

My mind grew fuzzy. I knew Gregory the Great was sometime after Constantine, which told me very little about this guy's artistic urges. Being a pope he probably had a hidden motive. Suddenly, I *saw* the answer from my art history textbook on page 118. I wrote with freedom: "Pope Gregory the Great believed that artistic images are useful for teaching laymen the holy word."

Ha!

I turned to the next question like a lion tamer facing a gerbil. "Rubens's 'Head of a Child' is probably the artist's: (a) oldest daughter (b) granddaughter (c) niece (d) youngest daughter." Normally I would have stabbed at something, but once again, the fantastic happened. My mind buzzed with the answer on page 415. I filled in "a" for oldest daughter and laughed.

"Ms. McCreary." It was Mr. Zeid. "Let's keep our chortling to ourselves, hmmmm?"

Right.

I sped through the test like it was a giant waterslide, keeping my chortling to myself. I'd never considered myself a candidate for a phenomenal memory, since I tend to blank on basics like where I put my car keys. I must have been studying subliminally all these months, and if I ever figured out how it worked I wasn't telling anyone.

I filled in the last box on the last page—"(c) from a tomb in Thebes, around 1400 B.C."—and sat back in exultation.

Chortle. Chortle.

Jonathan fluttered down from somewhere and sat on my desk. "You're welcome," he said.

Of course.

I smiled gratefully.

"I've been watching that Terris fellow," he said. "It could go either way."

My soul sank.

"His heart is hard," Jonathan explained. "That is one of the side effects you weren't interested in learning about yesterday. A hard heart is never promising, because it signals something deep and foreboding at the individual's root. I would not suggest going farther until we see the effect of—"

"*Please,*" I whispered, "go back and *do* something!"

Mr. Zeid caught that. "*Ms. McCreary,* would you care to share your enigmatic thoughts with the entire class?"

Never bring a cupid to school if you know what's good for you. I shook my head as Jonathan flitted.

Mr. Zeid pressed his Doomsday buzzer; the test was over. Glum students passed their papers forward and buried their heads in their hands.

"I advise against any action right now," Jonathan announced, and buzzed off.

Art History had ended. I told Mr. Zeid this was the finest test I'd ever had the privilege of taking. He sat down hard. I joined the teeming mass of Ben Franklin students thundering to sixth-period classes like lemmings bound for the sea. Peter Terris and Julia Hart were walking arm in arm in matching blue sweaters, oblivious to their surroundings. I approached them.

"Hi, guys," I chirped. "How are things in the Magic Kingdom?"

Jonathan zipped on the scene and hovered directly

in Peter's face to observe him. His wings beat quickly. He flew backward a foot, stopped, tilted, and pointed toward the ceiling. He took a small cluster of grapes from his quiver and began eating them. Julia looked at me with total, irritated shock; Peter broke into a wide, friendly grin and started laughing. Jonathan dived straight down and darted in and out between them, his brow furrowed. Peter kept laughing and said did I realize how funny I was? He'd see me around. I watched them leave.

Jonathan landed on my shoulder. "Still too early to tell," he said.

I ducked behind the sainted statue of Benjamin Franklin; angst surged through me. I gripped Ben's bronze boot. "I'm falling apart!" I wailed.

Jonathan eyed me somberly. "The human will is not easily broken, my friend. People are not robots."

"I don't want a robot! I want a boyfriend!"

"Everyone reacts differently to love," he added. "How Peter Terris reacts, we have no control over. That, my dear, was the piece of information you didn't care about earlier on!"

Three lowly freshmen had stopped to watch me shout and gesture to the air. I swung around.

"Do you mind?" I bellowed. They scattered like squirrels. I brushed off my jacket. Never underestimate the supremacy of senior year.

"A.J. . . ." It was Trish Beckman, looking Very

Worried. She was holding her psychology textbook open to chapter twenty-one—"Word Association."

"I'm going to say a word, A.J., and you say the first thing that comes into your mind. There are no wrong answers. Your subconscious will give us important clues so that we can get to the bottom of"—she winced—"your situation."

"I can't cope with this, Trish . . ."

"Mother," she said, her number-two pencil poised.

"Trish, please . . ."

"*Mother*. . . ," she insisted.

"Food," I said, sighing.

Trish shivered and wrote that down. "Father," she said.

"Cereal."

She sucked in a stream of air. I was flunking. "Love," she tried.

"Arrow," I said.

Trish considered my responses and said that she knew a fine psychiatrist in New Leonard who specialized in adolescent stress. She said she'd walk me to my next class because I shouldn't be alone. I patted her shoulder and said I'd manage, really, hoisted my book bag, and headed toward Oz. I leaned against the art-room door. It had a poster that read, ART IS THE DOOR WE OPEN TO UNDERSTAND OURSELVES. I tried opening the door; it was locked. Figures. Jonathan tapped his arrow on my book bag and hovered in my face.

"How," I muttered, "can something so small make me so crazy?"

"What?" Donny Krumper shrieked, frozen in my path. Donny was the smallest person at Ben Franklin High and took everything seriously.

"You think small people don't have feelings?" he bellowed.

"Donny, I wasn't talking to you, I was—"

"Sure!" Donny spat. *"Sure!* Walk all over small people! We're cute! We'll bounce back! You're going to get yours someday, McCreary!"

He stormed off, but it was clear I'd already gotten mine. Jonathan placed his arrow in his quiver and zoomed upward like a B-1 bomber.

I was sitting on the World Peace Bench in the Student Center contemplating the vicissitudes of life. This was not easy because the World Peace Bench was the most uncomfortable bench ever concocted: the back forced you forward, the seat forced you into contortions. It had been given to the school by last year's graduating class in the hope that everyone who sat on it would think about world peace. I shifted my weight and rubbed my lower back. The only thing I ever thought about when I sat on it was sitting somewhere else.

It was four o'clock; afternoon shadows crept across the Student Center. Jessica Wong hung a poster about the King of Hearts Dance that was five days away and stood back satisfied. She had a date. I'd never make the dance. I was so lame, I couldn't even get a guy to fall in love with me with a poisoned arrow. Nina Bloomfeld came by, shaken. She had just seen Eddie Royce, her rotten ex-boyfriend, with another girl. I motioned her to sit down. I patted her hand. I'd been there a hundred times.

She beat her fist in the air. "He cheated on me! He humiliated me! Who he dates shouldn't bother me! I should be celebrating that he's out of my life! Why, A.J., does it have to be so hard?"

I said I didn't know, but I knew how much it hurt. I had no idea how love even survived.

"Does it get better, A.J.? Does time heal?"

"Yes," I lied.

Nina nodded, lowered her head, and shuffled off. I leaned forward in despair. My parents were coming home tonight all lovey dovey, probably, from their weekend. They would ask how I was.

"Just ducky," I'd say.

Unloved.

Massively unappreciated.

"Hey, A.J.!"

I looked up.

"Over here!"

I looked up at the person who was waving at me with great emotion. I rubbed my eyes as he came closer. It couldn't be, but it *was*.

Peter Terris was running toward me!

My sinuses clogged with ecstasy. He was wearing sandy pants and a baby-blue sweater and he looked like a recruiting poster for Hunks from Heaven.

"How's it going?" he asked, smiling big and wide.

I shook off the cobwebs of despair. "Not bad . . ." I was breathing through my mouth.

He nodded and looked around. "So . . ." he said, grinning.

"So. . . ," I said, waiting.

"I was just thinking that . . ." He coughed.

Yes?

"Uh, it's kind of surprising, isn't it, A.J., that we've never gotten . . ." He stopped here and looked embarrassed.

I sat ramrod straight. Gotten *what*? Engaged, married . . .

"Gotten *together*," Peter said. "You know . . ."

I certainly did.

I crossed my leg nonchalantly and tried not to hyperventilate.

"Would you like to do that sometime—go out?"

I felt that answering by leaping into his arms would have been forward, so I said, "Sure," nice and casual and sat on my hands (they were shaking). I crossed my other leg, which had fallen asleep and now dangled from my thigh like a thick dead weight.

"Could I have your number?" he asked.

Could he?

Peter held out his English Lit textbook and a Bic and said to write it on the inside. I opened the book just as cool as could be. There were lots of phone numbers written there. My mind stopped.

"Your number," he said again.

I wrote 555; the pen went dry. I scratched it up and down to get the blasted ink moving, because Bic pens were never supposed to fail. Even if you forgot to take them out of your jeans and they ruined every last piece of decent clothing you had in the dryer, they went right on writing. Peter looked through his pocket. "I don't have another one," he said.

I tore open my purse, dug through Kleenex, antihistamine, nose spray, breath mints . . . no pen.

Peter looked down and cleared his throat as Julia Hart walked toward us, scowling.

"Just tell me," Peter said anxiously. "I'll remember."

"Five five five. . . ," I began.

"Yeah . . . ?"

"Five five five . . ." I blanked. I couldn't remember my own phone number! I knew it when I was in kindergarten; they wouldn't let you go home unless you did. Myra Tanninger couldn't remember hers and had it pinned to the inside of her coat in complete humiliation. I stood there like a massive stiff as Julia Hart walked faster and faster to claim what was unrightfully hers!

"Five five five," said a trusted voice behind me, "four two eight six." It was Trish Beckman, Best Friend in the Epic Pinch. I turned to her gratefully.

"I'll call you tonight," Peter said quietly, and walked quickly to Julia's curvaceous side.

He steered Julia past Big Ben, down the hall, past Mr. Zeid's room . . .

Trish turned to me, her mouth agape. "He approached you, A.J., in the presence of Death Incarnate!"

"He did, didn't he?"

Her eyes searched my face for uncurbed neurosis. She grabbed my arm. "My mother is waiting for me outside. I'm going to the dentist and will get Novocain and won't be able to speak, so I'll say it all now. *What is happening?*"

I grinned. "You're a wonderful friend, Trish."

"I want to know everything else!"

"I'll call you," I promised, and tried to look normal. "I'm fine now, Trish. That other stuff was—"

Her mother was honking the car horn like a hungry seal in the Fire Lane. "You are to call me, A.J., as soon as you hang up with him—the very second, do you understand? Don't go to the bathroom, don't stop for reflection, don't talk to yourself anywhere! It doesn't matter what time it is!"

CHAPTER EIGHT

I drove my Volvo home from school as only a truly desirable person can. I smiled at stranded motorists. I grinned at bad drivers. I drove past Comstock's Card Castle, past the Valentine cupids on display that had always seemed tired and inane until now.

I loved Valentine's Day!

I pulled into my happy two-car garage on top of which was my merry studio, and danced up the back steps to the kitchen, where Stieglitz, Boy Wonder Dog, greeted me in epic loyalty.

"Has anyone *called*, boy?" I danced to the phone and patted it. "Anyone gorgeous and witty and urbane?" Stieglitz had no idea, but took full advantage of my mood; he rolled on his back to have his stomach rubbed. I stroked his long, soft fur. "Wait till you meet him, boy! He is crazy about me!"

Stieglitz growled, sensing competition. I ran upstairs and pulled out the fabulous red dress I'd bought at retail for last year's King of Hearts Dance, the one I'd never worn because Robbie Oldsberg had dumped me two days before the dance and gone with Lisa Shooty, breaking my heart into a zillion pieces.

I put the dress on; the red silk hugged my body in all the right places—even my waist looked small. I pranced before my antique floor-mirror, a person in control of her destiny.

Take *that*, Robbie Oldsberg, you massive toad!

I turned from side to side, swishing my dress, shaking out my hair. I tore through my closet for the red heels with the little sequins (fifty percent off at Berringer's) that matched the dress perfectly. I squeezed into the shoes that were snug, did a little twirl, and raised my arms in victory.

Peter would call any minute, totally succumbed, and I would know devotion for the rest of my rich, full life.

The phone rang.

My heart stopped.

I let it ring three times because I didn't want to

seem anxious. I whispered an earthy hello. It was Trish, mumbling through Novocain displacement.

"Nothing yet," I said.

Trish garbled that she wouldn't sleep until I called, and hung up.

My stomach growled with anticipation—approaching ecstasy makes you hungry. I took off the dress and wrapped myself in my extra-large tartan robe and found microwavable sustenance in the kitchen—one of the perks of being the child of the Emotional Gourmet. I nuked a slab of herb bread and a container of Mom's drop-dead Chicken Paprikash. I washed this down with a bottle of Orangina and two cherry fritters. The phone rang again. I counted two rings this time, not wanting to push my luck, and breathed my sexiest hello.

"*Mrs. McCreary,*" said the pushy voice. "And how are you this evening?"

"I'm not Mrs.—"

"Stan Hurlehan, *Mrs. McCreary,* of the Triple A Siding Company, with a special offer that could change your life!"

Keeping the phone line free was the only thing that could change my life. I said I was waiting for an emergency call. Good-bye.

It was eight-eighteen; Peter still hadn't called. Maybe he was injured. I did the direct, today's assertive female thing: called his house, heard his voice, and hung up. Calling had to be *his* idea. I glared at the phone:

"*Ring!*" I shouted.

It didn't.

Peter was *home*; worse than that, Peter was home and not calling me!

I hadn't walked Stieglitz. I hadn't done my homework. I hadn't figured out what I would say to my parents when, in one hour, they would be landing at LaGuardia Airport, fresh from two fun-packed days and nights in New Orleans. I hadn't exercised in days; I ran up and down three flights of stairs for thirty minutes, which kept me in the presence of the Nonringing Phone. I curled into a lump, wheezing on the kitchen floor, and wondered if I could get arrested for manipulation. I shook creeping angst from my soul and made the wedding list, keeping it just under three hundred on my side with only eight bridesmaids. Trish called again and said she was just checking the phone line.

"Ring!" I shouted at the blasted phone.

It did; I yanked it off the wall. *"Hello!"* I shrieked.

"A.J.," said the golden voice of my dreams . . .

"Speaking. . . ," I crooned.

"This is—"

"Peter. . . ," I said dreamily.

"I have to see you," he nearly shouted. "Something's happened . . . I can't explain."

Love is like that.

"Can I come over, A.J.? Please?"

"Yes, Peter! I'm free! I live at—"

"I know where you live!"

Right.

I kissed the phone. *It was happening!* I ran upstairs to become gorgeous, although with Jonathan's arrow trick I could probably answer the door in arctic slipper socks and a sack and nothing would deter Peter's heart. But I wanted to give him a good show when he scooped me up in his arms.

At least that's what I thought he would do.

Succumbed people act normally, right?

A small knot twisted in my stomach. I put on my lavender sweater that made me look sexy but sincere, and brushed out my hair until it shone and flounced with honesty. Truth seemed to be a recurring theme as I was getting dressed.

Guilt trickled over me. I'd been anything but honest.

I'd been selfish, corrupt . . .

Jonathan hovered down from the ceiling, eating a carrot.

"Where . . . have you been?" I stammered.

"Observing," he said gravely.

Jonathan's dark, dinky eyes looked right through me. I brushed off my sweater that didn't need it and looked furtively out the window.

"Why are you frightened?" he asked.

"I'm not frightened!" I swallowed hard as panic rose in my chest.

What would Peter do when he got here?

"You must listen to the things that you try to ignore," Jonathan intoned.

I jumped as a honk and a screech sounded on the street. Stieglitz went positively ballistic in his death-to-intruders dance and flashed his jaws. I looked out the window and tingled as Peter's souped-up Jeep tore up the driveway and *he* jumped out in epic perfection. I felt my kidneys curl. Then my parents' car pulled up alongside him.

I closed my eyes; it was going to be an interesting evening.

There was no time to prepare my parents to meet their future son-in-law.

"I hope," Jonathan said solemnly, "that you enjoy the dance."

I shuddered and walked downstairs, part of me exulting, the other part nauseous. Peter was introducing himself to my mother, then he shook my father's hand like he was priming an old pump. I made my big entrance, taking the steps slow because I was shaking. He was wearing a navy-blue turtleneck and brushed jeans— I go crazy for males in turtlenecks. His eyes locked with mine—he was a gonner. Stieglitz was barking like a mad fiend, running up and down the stairs, killing the mood.

"Stop it!" I hissed. Stieglitz darted in front of me, I tripped over his hind legs, plummeted three stairs down, and crashed, once again, at Peter's supreme feet.

Peter picked me up. "A.J.!" he cried, devastated. "Are you all right?"

If I'd taken ballet, this never would have happened. I brushed myself off. Stieglitz growled at Peter like he was president of the Dog Catchers Union. Peter gazed at me like a Doberman contemplating sirloin.

My parents stood rigid in the hall, holding their luggage, trying, as all parents of teenagers attempt through the ages, to read between the lines. I turned to them and smiled bleakly.

"Mom, Dad, how nice to see you. I'm perfectly fine. The house is fine. How was your trip? Did you have a nice flight? You're right on time, I see. Isn't this nice? Oh . . . this is Peter, a guy from school."

"We've met," said Dad, unsure.

"It's a bit late for a visit, isn't it?" asked Mom, shifting her carry-on bag. She was gearing up to say a mouthful.

Mom, Dad, and Peter smiled anxiously at each other as Stieglitz bared his teeth. I glared at my parents like maybe this would be a good time for them to leave us alone, all things considered. Then, just as charming as anything, Peter said, "Mr. and Mrs. McCreary, I apologize for the hour. It must seem irresponsible of me. I just needed to say something to A.J. and then I'll go."

Mom and Dad sifted his words, not blinking.

"I don't want to do anything to give you a bad opinion of me," Peter added, smiling at my parents with absolute charm. "I'm sorry if I've pushed the rules. Would it be okay if I spoke to A.J. for one moment?"

Mom smiled back, which meant she was melting. Dad hadn't blinked yet. Mom jabbed Dad in the ribs and pulled him toward the kitchen.

"Ten minutes," she said with a grin.

"Five," Dad countered.

Peter waited until the kitchen door closed. I was dying. I'd memorized every inch of him; I'd photographed him from every angle; and now he was here!

"Strict parents," Peter said finally, rolling his eyes.

"They're not strict, they're . . ." I let it pass. Stieglitz didn't; he pawed the carpet and showed his teeth.

"Hey, there, dog," said Peter stretching out his gorgeous hand. Stieglitz flashed fangs and nipped him.

"Bad dog!" I shoved Stieglitz into the kitchen, ran back to Peter, and attended his wound.

"I'm so sorry . . . he's never done that . . . he's . . ."

"It doesn't matter," Peter whispered, caressing my hand.

"It doesn't?" I gulped hard, grabbing the banister with the other one for strength.

"Can't feel a thing," he insisted, drawing me close.

I could feel everything.

Peter nuzzled my cheek; my jaw started quivering.

He pulled me closer; my knees gave way. His breath was hot on my neck and I could feel the beating of his heart, like it was trying to jump out of his chest right into mine. Then he kissed me—it was like sinking in something soft, like losing all of yourself in a glorious moment in time. He kept kissing me and I kept holding on. I took a deep breath so I wouldn't faint.

Stieglitz went ape behind the kitchen door. I remembered where I was.

"Peter," I whispered breathlessly, checking the kitchen door for my parents, "you said there was something you wanted to say?"

He grinned, stepped back, and gazed at me with total adoration. "It happened at dinner," he said. "I was eating meat loaf and . . . suddenly I saw your face . . ."

"In the meatloaf . . ."

"In my mind!" His eyes were wild and gauzy.

"Yes?"

"And I realized I . . ."

"Yes?"

"I . . . well . . . I felt this shot through my heart like . . ."

Jonathan was hovering halfway down the stairs, observing Peter like a scientist watches a laboratory rat.

"And," Peter continued, *"I just knew you were the one!"*

Ecstasy!

I reached out to hug him. None of the other boys were like this. No love had ever been like this!

Jonathan folded his arms, waiting.

Then Peter's eyes cleared. He stepped back, he looked around confused.

"What . . . ?" he shook his head. He glared at me like I was the worst news of his life and backed off.

"What," Peter demanded, "am I doing here?"

"Huh?"

Jonathan fluttered right in Peter's face and looked into his eyes.

"What," Peter shouted, *"is going on?"*

"You called me," I reminded him. "You said it was urgent!"

"What are you talking about?"

"Yes"—I was deflated—*"you did!"* I stared at Jonathan, who was flying in zigzag patterns around Peter's head and chest. "You said you were eating meat loaf and . . ." I stopped here because it was clear he didn't remember.

"I've got to go home," Peter said nervously, lunging toward the door. "I think I'm sick."

He tore down the great stone steps like a hunted animal.

"Peter! Wait!"

But it was no use. Peter slammed his Jeep out of the driveway and screeched off.

I crumbled in the hall on terra cotta tiles.

"Most peculiar," Jonathan said solemnly, landing on the banister. "I have never observed this reaction before."

"He was here!" I wailed. "We were so close! *And now he's gone forever!*"

I ran upstairs and crashed on my futon in tears.

Chapter Nine

I lay on my futon, a broken shell.

Peter Terris couldn't stand me! I slammed my head in my nonallergenic pillow and wept bitterly.

My parents had come up earlier, wondering what was wrong.

"Nothing," I sobbed, which they didn't buy.

"Everything," I tried again. But I couldn't talk about it except to say that I was giving up the entire male species because I was an abject failure at romance, and they should probably forget about ever having grandchildren.

"We won't hold you to that, honey," said my mother.

I curled into the fetal position and said I needed to be alone. They muttered parental concerns and left.

I called Trish because I'd promised I would; when you can't even spear a boyfriend with mythology, you need to cling to those precious relationships mired in history.

"It was a consummate bust," I groaned to her, *"beyond* torture. I can't even talk about it now. We're over; we never even began . . ."

Trish mumbled from the good side of her mouth that she was really sorry. I said we'd talk tomorrow, I said she was a great friend, I said that life had no meaning, and hung up.

I sighed with the depth only known to the unrequited-love professional. I remembered a conversation I'd had with Mr. Zeid last February after Robbie Oldsberg dumped me. I'd been trying to photograph the pain I was feeling, trying to communicate abandonment through my art, but instead of connecting with that, my photographs were stagnant. Mr. Zeid reminded me that it took Michelangelo eons to finish the ceiling for the Sistine Chapel, to record correctly what he'd seen and felt. I pointed out that Michelangelo got back problems from the entire ordeal, not to mention major papal stress, to which Mr. Zeid delivered his singsong line that he used to zonk every crop of new Art History students:

"Every artist, somewhere, somehow, has to suffer. It is the strength of art itself that brings greatness and beauty out of chaos."

I said if suffering was a prerequisite to greatness, my name was going to be a household word.

I pulled my quilt around me tight as Stieglitz peeked into my room, still devastated that I'd called him a *bad dog*. His tail was lowered.

"It's okay, boy."

Stieglitz sighed with relief and climbed on the futon. I rubbed his head and felt like an evil genie.

Trying to make someone do something he didn't want to do was monstrous. God was punishing me and I deserved it. I remembered a Bible story I'd learned years ago in Sunday school about King Solomon. God made Solomon king and asked Solomon what he wanted most. Solomon said wisdom and God said, good choice, and gave it to him with everything else you could imagine. Mrs. Pilson, my Sunday school teacher, said that God rewarded Solomon because he had asked wisely. Billy Haggamon said *he* would have asked to own the Lionel Train Company. Mrs. Pilson said she was quite certain God wouldn't give Billy the choice.

I had had a choice.

A rich, magical, life-changing choice.

And I had gone the way of Billy Haggamon.

I had blown it!

The phone rang; it was the siding man, probably,

looking to change my life. I reached for the receiver and managed a bleak hello.

"A.J.!" said the voice.

I bolted up.

"A.J., it's Peter! Can you ever forgive me?"

Hope soared through me.

"I just got home, A.J., and I can't believe I walked out like that! I don't know what's the matter with me, I must be sick or something!"

He said he was sorry a hundred times; he'd been feeling strange, he explained. He'd never, he promised, ever act like that again.

Peter said he wanted to drive me to school in the morning; I curled on my futon in a happy ball. I pictured us snuggled together in the front seat of his brown Jeep, screeching up to school as an official dating unit. I saw Julia Hart's face drop in green-eyed envy as Peter and I paraded in matching sweaters down the Benjamin Franklin parking lot promenade that only popular students swish down, since it was in full view of the entire world. Popular students don't worry about tripping, or burping dementedly in public—popular students are immune from life's social spasms.

Then he said he wanted to drive me to school *every* morning, as in *forever*!

Joy shot through me. *Yes,* I shouted, he could drive me! His mother picked up the phone at this point and told him to get off and get some sleep—a real mood killer, but not even parental boorishness could extinguish our eternal flame. He said he'd see me tomorrow. He said he'd think about me tonight. Then he said he probably wouldn't sleep much for all the thinking he was going to do about me, and I swear, if I could have jumped through the receiver into his gorgeous lap at that moment, I would have.

Peter said he didn't think he could wait until tomorrow and I said I didn't think I could either. That's when his mother picked up the receiver and screamed, *"Now!"* like a supreme shrew. I vowed then and there that I would never be like that when Peter and I had children. I would never forget, even in my ancient, aged state, what it was like to be seventeen.

I hung up feeling like I'd just sunk into warm fudge and threw a pillow into the air because I had to do something expansive. The pillow hit my desk lamp, which crashed to the floor with great emotion.

I knelt down to pick up broken light-bulb pieces. There was a knock on my door and my mother walked in.

"I heard a crash," she said.

"A crash of victory, Mother!"

"Are you all right?"

"I am absolutely wonderful, Mother! Life has taken a rich new turn!"

Mom knelt down to help me and threw broken glass into the wastebasket. "Specifics would help, honey."

"Peter and I are together again. He called and everything is perfect!"

Mom put the lamp back on my desk, dissecting my words. "Tell me about Peter," she said finally.

I went for the Cliffs Notes version. "He's the most fabulous male in the universe, Mother! He is *the* best boy at school—not even Todd Kovich at his pinnacle, before he became a total buzzard, could beat him. He is brilliant and wonderful and *he's crazy about me!*"

"I've missed a lot being in New Orleans." Mom sat on a chair, because her forty-four-year-old knees were going. "When did you start seeing each other?"

I cleared my throat at this point. Of course, I wanted to tell her everything—however, everything was a politically incorrect move that could cause me to lose certain privileges, like my future, since telling my mother about Jonathan would get me committed, and who knew what Jonathan would do? So I said, "Today . . . kind of . . ." good and fast, and gave her time to get used to the concept.

She took off her glasses. *"Today?"*

"Things had been building . . ."

She stared at me through tired eyes.

"True love, Mother, is not bound by time."

"I see."

"True love is something that you have to trust your instincts about, and sometimes those instincts get buried, you know, even though they're there, and then one day . . . splat . . . they gush out . . . like striking oil . . ."

"You've been gushing most of the day, then?"

I looked down. "Pretty much . . ." I wasn't sure the gushing metaphor was helping.

"And Peter? He's been gushing too?"

"Uh . . . on and off . . . you know . . ."

Mom picked up from my dresser the little crystal dog that Todd Kovich had given me when we were achingly in love. She examined it for clues. "Then why," asked Mom, poised for truth, "were you crying?"

I stiffened, because that wasn't the point. I wasn't crying *now*. "It was a momentary lapse, Mother, everything is fine now—massively flawless. You and Dad won't have to worry about me ever again."

She took this in. "Your father will be relieved."

"It's been a decent day."

Mom measured her next words carefully. I figured she had three minutes left before she folded. "I don't want you to misinterpret what I'm about to say."

I froze in misunderstanding.

"*Or* be defensive."

I folded my arms tight.

"I'm glad you've got a guy you really like, A.J., but I think you need to walk very carefully."

"*Mother,* I'm—"

"You *need,*" she said, gaining strength, "to look at this relationship with clear eyes—"

"You don't even know him, Mother, and—"

"But I know *you*," she said. "And I've seen the frustrations you've gone through with other relationships because your heart gets in the way of your mind and you close yourself off to the truth about people."

I was ripped, but said nothing.

"Todd Kovich," she reminded me, putting the crystal dog down, "wasn't a nice guy."

"I'd appreciate it, Mother, if you would never utter his name in my presence . . ."

"You knew the games he'd played with other girls; you saw firsthand how he used and manipulated relationships. You knew who he was, A.J., when you went out with him."

"I don't want to talk about this now . . ."

"I know you don't . . . but we need to talk about it because the same thing happened with Robbie Oldsberg and Scott Zimmerman and Don Lucetti with that great cleft chin. I don't want you to leap into another relationship without thinking. Looking for perfect is a big, fat myth because *perfect* isn't out there."

That was rich coming from my mother, the Emotional Gourmet of Crestport, Connecticut, who had been known to slave for hours trying to perfect her Candied Claret Pears that guests would consume in eleven minutes flat. I had seen her throw out cakes that were a half an inch too short and sneer at any zucchini that wasn't seven inches long and perfectly tapered. I wanted to shout that perfection sure seemed to run in the family, and that I, for one, could have it without guilt and pain. All it took was a little arrow flying through space and a reverberating *thwonk*.

"I'm in the perfection business," Mom said quietly. "The food *always* has to look great or I'm dead. I have to keep reminding myself that in the people business, perfection trips you up. The funny thing is, honey, if you ever did get a totally perfect guy, he would make you miserable."

Jonathan peered at me from my purple hat rack.

"Lecture's over," Mom said, giving me a hug. "Get some sleep."

She got up slowly and paused at the door like she had more to say. She didn't say it, though—just tapped the door lovingly and padded off to bed.

"Your mother," said Jonathan, floating down, "is a wise woman."

I hugged my knees. Mom was operating on earth wisdom. I, on the other hand . . .

Jonathan perched on the little crystal dog and regarded it coldly.

"Listen," I began, "I really want to thank you for what you've done." Jonathan folded his wings and looked down. "I'm happy, Jonathan, for the first time in eons!"

He gazed sadly out the window; his little body went taut. "You will sleep," he said flatly.

. . .

Peter picked me up at 7:17 A.M. in his brown Jeep with tan interior—he was all lovesick smiles. He handed Stieglitz a Milk-Bone in friendship, but Stieglitz still hated him. He told me I looked beautiful. I was wearing my quilted green jacket, black jeans, and a patterned yellow Tee. He grabbed my father by the shoulders and shouted, "Mr. McCreary, it is *so* great to see you!" Dad drank a mug of hot coffee in one gulp.

"Well," I said, yanking Peter out the door, "have a nifty day, Dad."

I settled into the Jeep, wondering if Peter would turn into a werewolf; he didn't. He sweetly handed me a freshly baked blueberry muffin. He talked about being on the debate team and complimented my outfit. He said he couldn't believe that we'd never gone out all these years and that he must have been blind. He held my hand and didn't get nuts. He said I was wonderful. He said he wished it was Saturday so we could be together all day. He said he'd never felt like this and that more than anything he wanted to park this stupid Jeep and hold me. My heart was pumping and my hands were shaking and I said that would be really fine with me. He pulled the Jeep over and cradled me with gentleness, kissed my head, and asked if I was going to the King of Hearts Dance with anyone.

"Not yet," I cooed.

"Would you like to go with me?"

He was breaking the rules—girls asked guys to this dance—but rules were meaningless to the supremely succumbed. I nuzzled his cheek and said I would. A certain winged being appeared out of nowhere and buzzed around us like a mechanic checking a stalled car. I was truly grateful to Jonathan for having zapped Peter with undying devotion, but he was bludgeoning a tender moment. I signaled for him to leave; he didn't. Peter looked at me strangely. I swatted the air near Jonathan for effect. A shaft of sunshine flashed across his quiver as he did a triple aerial loop and zipped out of the way.

"A . . . fly," I explained to Peter.

Jonathan said "Hmmmph" at being called a fly and looked in Peter's ear, which was killing the mood. He peered into Peter's ice-green eyes, took a tuft of Peter's hair, rubbed it in his fingers, perched on top of the steering wheel, and said, "Looks normal. I can't explain it."

Then go away!

Jonathan waited. Peter put his hand over his chest and bent down. "I just had this funny twinge," he said.

"Most bewildering," said Jonathan, flying backward right out the window.

. . .

I was standing in the Student Center by the statue of Big Ben, waiting for Peter, who had dropped me off right in front of school, so I wouldn't have to walk across the cold, slushy parking lot. I was gazing at Ben in all his bronzeness—a jack-of-all-trades, who'd accomplished things because he had had vision. A big red bow was draped under his chin, courtesy of the King of Hearts Dance Committee; a pair of pantyhose dangled from his outstretched hand. Imagine what that man could have done with a cupid.

"You don't have to thank me now, A.J.," said Trish Beckman, running up beside me. "You can take your time about doing that, picking the appropriate thank-you gift, which, would be altogether appropriate, because I, your best friend, am about to change your life."

"What are you talking about?"

"I know you were mortally wounded by Peter Terris being a chump last night, but he's a killer, A.J., who can't be tamed. What I'm about to tell you requires immediate action!" She touched her right cheek that was swollen from dental distress. "Alex DuMont just broke up with Cassie McLaughlin!"

"Yeah . . . ?"

"This is not rumor, A.J., I saw the whole thing. He asked for his ring back *and* his jacket right by the World Peace Bench. It was like she was getting kicked out of the army. He took it all, A.J., and said she'd cheated on him, which she had—everyone saw her at the Pizza Pavilion with Bobby Pershing."

I said, "That's too bad," and looked down the hall for Peter.

"A.J.!" Trish cried. "Alex DuMont is available and angry! He's likely to say yes to anything at this point!"

"Even me?"

"That's not what I meant. You ask Alex to the dance, and I"—she took a deep breath—"will ask Tucker before I lose my nerve. On the count of three . . ."

"I'm going to pass, Trish."

"But Alex DuMont is *darling*!"

"I already have a boyfriend."

"*Who?*"

I smiled, and said, "Peter Terris," nice and slow.

Her mouth dropped open: *"When did this happen?"*

"Last night."

"You didn't call!"

"I called the first time . . ."

"We always call if anything changes!"

"I was tired. I was trying to sort things out."

"Tell me everything!"

I wanted to. I wanted to confess it all. Peter ran up to meet me and put his arm tight around my shoulder. I waved to Trish, whose tongue was flapping. "It's okay," I said to her, then whispered, "Close your mouth."

She didn't.

I put my arm around Peter's waist so you couldn't tell where one of us ended and the other began, and we eased on down the hall, an official dating unit. I waved good-bye to Trish, my dear confused friend, who had turned into a stone statue.

I'd make it up to her somehow after she'd melted.

School with Peter by my side was exhilarating. We held hands. We snuggled. We exchanged locker combinations. Every nerve in me was alive to love. I shivered when he took my hand. My breath stopped when he kissed the top of my head—just stuck there really heavy before it got to my throat and I wondered if I would ever breathe again. He waited for me outside every class. When I got within feet of him it was like everyone else went away and I started grinning like a dodo and he was grinning too.

We sent shock waves through Ben Franklin High. Pearly saw us and positively gaped. Julia Hart saw us and turned bright crimson. She marched angrily up to Peter.

"May I speak to you, *please*?" she demanded.

Peter looked at her like she was a gnat. "Not now, Julia."

She backed off, powerless.

This boy had succumbed!

At the sound of every bell we rushed from the prison of our classes to each other's side. We ached, we hungered. It was pointless being in school, the waste of two perfectly good desks. Each time Peter looked at me there was more love in his eyes. Everyone could see it. I had several sneezing fits and he gave me his handkerchief. A senior boy who carried his own handkerchief! For an allergic person this was the ultimate.

We entered the Inner Sanctum of the Student Center, where the "in" seniors gather—it was right by the coldest water fountain and no one dared go there unless they were important. There was Melissa Pageant, who had never invited me to any of her parties; there was Al Costanzo, Star Running Back, who didn't know I was alive. There was Lisa Shooty, Head Cheerleader, bouncing away. There was Heidi Morganthaller, who had stolen Scott Zimmerman from under my nose when I had the stomach flu and couldn't fight back except to throw up on her, which I'd considered. Peter pushed the water faucet button for me and I drank. The water *was* colder.

Melissa Pageant eyed me up and down.

We stared at each other like cats do right before they start fighting. *Get used to it,* I felt like saying, but Peter steered me away.

We walked to Mr. Zeid's room for my seventh-period *Oracle* meeting. It was like tooling down a busy road in a brand-new Ferrari. Everyone looked. Everyone was jealous right down to their toes. Then the jealousy moved into consummate respect. I took a deep breath of the Big Time.

I was somebody!

Students parted for us as we walked by. A football player ogled me. I felt a glow of importance as Peter kissed me on the cheek and jogged off to gym class. I leaned back on Mr. Zeid's door, positively dizzy.

Trish pounced on me.

"Explain to me, A.J., what's happening, please! Julia Hart has gone into apoplexy! Peter Terris is hanging on to you like you're a winning Lotto ticket!"

I took a deep, guilty breath. Trish and I told each other everything; I was holding back, breaking the supreme bond of best-friendship. Of course she'd done this once, too, during sophomore year when we both liked Nathan Lawler (who was *my* type, not hers), and she denied it right up to the Saturday night when she went out with him behind my back, and felt so guilty about it that she called me from the movie theater to confess. Nathan's father got transferred to Baltimore and he moved that semester, which meant we didn't have to see him in the hall and pretend that a mere male had almost destroyed our friendship. Trish, who was five three, went back to liking short, stocky wrestlers, and I continued my search for the perfect, gangly male. Trish and I have seen the worst in each other and decided to hang out anyway.

The bell rang; Trish looked through me. *"Well?"* she shouted.

I couldn't tell her anything now. So I made a joke and hid behind it. "When you're hot, you're hot," I said.

Trish felt my forehead.

"He likes me. What can I say?"

Pearly danced into Mr. Zeid's room at this point, all smiles.

She was holding a poster and a box of folders.

"Hello! Hello!" Pearly chirped out of character.

"Why is she smiling?" Trish demanded, looking nervous. *"What is happening to everyone?"*

CHAPTER TEN

"Attention, everyone, please!"

Carl Yolanta and Tucker Crawford looked up from their SAVE THE WORLD fliers as Pearly Shoemaker stood regally before us and held up a poster-sized blow-up of my soon-to-be award-winning photograph, "Donna Is Confused." She had chosen the shot without the pigeon.

"Our cover," she announced proudly. "Courtesy of A. J. McCreary."

There was silence at first as the *Oracle* staff read of

Donna's trials with Steve, Gary, Derek, and Nathaniel. Then mouths broke into grins, grins turned to laughs. I smiled proudly. We *were* all Donna—except that now I wasn't confused anymore.

"I think I can speak for everyone, A.J., when I say that you have truly outdone yourself."

The group applauded.

"And now," Pearly continued, "we have confirmation that our Valentine edition is going all the way to the top!"

We looked at each other as Pearly whipped out a folder and took out a full-page ad of a perfect couple running on the beach holding Pepsis and not spilling them.

"Pepsi," she whispered, "has come to Crestport."

Everyone oohed and aahed except Tucker, who was allergic to hype.

"Pepsi," Pearly continued, "has caught *my* vision." She sat down, overcome. "With help from Erin Donner, whose mother is on the Pepsi account team. Thank you, Erin." Erin smiled and looked embarrassed.

"What exactly does this mean?" asked Tucker, tapping his pen.

Pearly stared at him, appalled. "It *means,* Tucker, that a national advertiser has embraced the concept of love and today's teen!"

Tucker examined the Pepsi ad. "Let me get this straight, Pearly. If Pepsi hadn't bought an ad you're saying we wouldn't be a success?"

Pearly closed her mascaraed eyes. "I'm *saying,* Tucker, that Pepsi's sponsorship is impressive."

"They make sugared water and put it in cans."

"They are a major force in the world!" Pearly fumed.

Tucker made a sound like a mule. "I get the feeling, Pearly, that we're all part of your game here. I mean, what's the point of this Valentine edition? You want to do something on teenage love? Let's talk *real issues,* not soda pop!"

Tucker was angry most of the time, which would serve him well as an investigative reporter later in life. He said the *Oracle* was becoming a farce and dared her to publish an article he had just written on being alone. "You can't be with someone else effectively, unless you can stand to be alone with yourself," he declared. "Being part of a couple isn't the final answer. It can't define who you are."

I thought being part of an enchanted twosome beat the pants off learning to be alone with yourself. Those of us present knew Tucker was not a winner in the love and romance department, since he insisted that his girlfriends be rabid about his latest causes. Trish beamed at him, ready to take up the gauntlet.

"So are you gonna publish my article, Pearly?" Tucker asked. "Put it as the lead story right up front to offset McCreary's cover?"

Carl Yolanta gave Tucker a friendly punch. "It's a good cover," he said.

Pearly said she'd see as I smiled at Carl, the Ultimate Nice Guy. I knew better than to box with Tucker, because he never gave up, especially when he was wrong. He was the perfect one to write about being alone, given his track record. Pearly said we'd all done a boffo job, the Valentine edition was coming out Friday to stun and amaze a needy world. She adjourned the meeting fast.

Tucker walked up to Trish and said, "We're too busy as a society to take the time to get to know ourselves. We're running from this to that and not getting anywhere." Trish looked at him dreamily and said she absolutely agreed. He shot her a thin smile and she melted. Tucker started off in his fast, investigative-reporter gait, then doubled back to walk with Trish. Trish walked slowly when she was in love and it took them half the hall to click into a unified gait.

Peter was waiting for me in deep yearning.

"A.J.," he said adoringly.

"Peter," I said breathlessly.

Peter took possession of my hand. We glided through the puke-green halls of Ben Franklin High, basking in softly diffused light. We were enveloped in the Student Center. Lisa Shooty invited us to her post King of Hearts Dance party. Barry Lund, the senior class president, asked if we wanted to double-date. Sara Fizinowski eyed me with consummate covetousness and asked where I got my quilted jacket. Robbie Oldsberg stared at me with new eyes, realizing what he'd lost.

Hello, I felt like shouting, *remember me? I'm the one you never noticed before . . .*

I made my way to the bathroom and was standing at the sink; a small freshman girl stared at me like I was famous. I stood up straight and shook out my hair (she did this too). I flounced my blouse over my belt (so did she). I put on lip gloss (she reached for hers). I put my F2 over my shoulder (she didn't have one).

I strode confidently out the door, awed by my power.

Jonathan fluttered down from the ceiling vent. "How are the lovebirds?" he asked.

I'd learned my lesson. I wasn't going to gesture or speak to the air like a moron. I epoxied myself to Peter's gorgeous side and beamed.

Then suddenly Peter's face went morbidly pale. He bent over and clutched his heart.

"Peter!"

"I just had this . . . sharp pain. . . ," he stammered, trying to straighten. He caught his breath. "I'm okay," he said shakily. "It's gone."

I grabbed his hand. Jonathan put his ear on Peter's chest, listening. I said it was gas, maybe. Heartburn. I said I was really sorry. I looked at Jonathan who looked at Peter like Dr. Frankenstein looked at his monster.

"We will hope for the best," Jonathan said gravely, and flew off.

I was hoping for the best, hoping so hard that my hope muscles hurt. Peter and I huddled behind Big Ben, trying to steal a few quiet moments.

Lisa Shooty grinned her Head Cheerleader smile at me and bounced over. Lisa had never given me the time of day. She tossed her mane of flawless raven curls and patted my F2 like it was a stuffed animal.

"A.J.," she cooed, "I have so wanted a really great photo of myself as Head Cheerleader leading cheers at a game . . ." She let her hand glide over my camera. "I was hoping that you, who are the greatest photographer any of us knows, would take it." She smiled extra hard.

I smiled too, the way Mom taught me to when a customer was being a pain.

"I just don't want a *strange* picture, A.J. . . ."

"You mean like the one I took of the football team growling and caked with mud?"

She nodded.

"You want something, Lisa, that captures passion, school spirit, and that really great backflip you do at halftime when your skirt goes up?"

She grabbed my arm. "You understand, A.J.— cheerleading is very centering for me."

The plaintive sound of a lone kazoo wailed from the front of the Student Center. All eyes turned to see

Gary Quark, chairman of the King of Hearts Dance Committee, dressed in a purple robe and crown. Katie Broadringer, dressed like a Valentine heart, did a cartwheel in front of Gary, who blew his kazoo again.

"Hear ye, hear ye!" Gary cried. "Let it be known that the King of Hearts Dance is only four days away!" A ripple of anxiety gripped the air as dateless girls considered their prospects.

"So if you haven't asked him yet"—Gary paused here for royal impact as Katie did a series of happy-heart somersaults—"*do it*! I myself was only picked off last week." He smiled at Becca Loadstrom, who had done the picking.

"*And*"—Gary raised his plastic scepter—"you have only two more days to cast your votes for that macho senior male who will wear this crown as *the* King of Hearts!" Gary took the crown off his head and waved it. I smiled proudly at Peter—his chances of being crowned King were excellent. Only Al Costanzo could possibly beat him. Gary gave a final snort on his kazoo. Katie did a cartwheel and ended in a heartrending split. They exited to polite applause.

I leaned back on Peter's kingly shoulder. We would knock the world on its ear Saturday night.

Wednesday I was sitting with Peter on his sister's couch as his destructive two-year-old niece, Marcie, dive-bombed the ottoman with her plastic doll. We were going to have pizza while he baby-sat Marcie, a task his mother forced upon him to keep the family together. Peter stroked my hand; our hearts beat as one. Marcie stuck her tongue out at me and wiped glop on my supremely expensive cowl-neck sweater that I had bought to impress Peter's mother, who was grinning at Marcie like she was the most adorable child in the world. I eyed Marcie's glop and smiled tolerantly just like Mom did when Dad's aunt Agnes asked her why she spent so much time cooking for other people when she should be at home cooking for *us*. Marcie made a foul noise meant for me. I didn't kill her. I was trying to make a good impression.

Peter's sister, Sarah, was dashing about in a violet silk suit while Marcie tried to rub a Hershey's kiss on as much of her mother as possible. Peter's mother was tall and stylish and exhibited no further supreme shrew characteristics. She said I must be a very special girl because all Peter had been talking about for the last few days was me. Sarah's husband, Hector, was a gastro-enterologist who carried a clip-on phone and ate Tums.

"Sarah," Hector barked, "get the seat and let's go!"

By "the seat" Hector meant Marcie's new potty chair that was pink and happy and played "Somewhere Over the Rainbow" at the vaguest hint of moisture. Sarah plunked the seat down.

"She's not . . . trained?" I asked, gulping.

"We're working on it," chirped Sarah. "Marcie's a very big girl and we know she can do it!"

Marcie kicked the seat and toddled away.

Sarah handed Peter a bag of Hershey's kisses that were Marcie's rewards when she used the chair. "It's the learn-by-doing method," Sarah explained. "Instant rewards, instant gratification. They train themselves. Just have the doll wet first; you'll be fine." Sarah beamed at Marcie who was eyeing the candy bag. "Kiss Mommy good-bye, sweetie."

Marcie lunged for a Hershey's kiss instead of her mother; Peter tossed the bag to me. I threw it on the stereo as Sarah, Hector, and Mrs. Terris hurried out the door to meet Mr. Terris in the city. Mr. Terris was a personal-injury lawyer and always worked late. I guess you never know when tragedy might strike.

Marcie made a noise like a B-52 and rammed her doll into the stereo cabinet. She stormed up to me and shoved the doll in my face.

"Make dolly wet!" she demanded.

Peter groaned. I took Marcie and the doll into the bathroom, unscrewed the doll's head, poured water inside the plastic body, and put the head back on. "There," I said, "you make the dolly wet." I was going to add "in the next county," but decided against it.

Marcie ran back to the living room, sat the doll on the pink potty chair, and squeezed its stomach viciously. Streams of water squirted into the bowl, causing the chair to play "Somewhere Over the Rainbow" and Marcie to shriek, "Good dolly!" Peter handed her a Hershey's kiss, which she smeared around the doll's mouth before devouring it herself.

"Well," I said, "so this is potty training."

I gazed at Peter's sculpted jaw. Over the weekend we were going to merge our CD collections, which was almost like being engaged. We had perfection right down to coordination in pizza toppings (we both adored veggie). This was an absolute sign from heaven that our love would last. We'd be munching Veggie Supremos when we were gnarled and middle aged. But antiquity was light years away. The Dance of the Century was almost upon us.

The whole school felt its power. All anyone could get out of the King of Hearts Dance Committee was a knowing smile and a whispered assurance that *this dance* was going to blow the prom out of the water. Everyone who went would be changed forever; everyone who sat home would ache for what could have been. It would be my moment in the sun, the deliverance from years of grinding pathos and romantic devastation.

We cuddled close as Marcie whacked the chair. Not even potty training could extinguish our eternal flame. There was so much we had to learn about each other, so much distance that had separated our empty lives until now. I wanted to know every last scrumptious fact about him.

"Peter, tell me about the debate team."

Peter shrugged. "It's okay."

"I mean *really* tell me. I want to know what it's like in the heat of a debate when the clock is ticking and you're up there and the whole team is counting on you to say something brilliant and the other guy has just scored a big point."

He shrugged.

"Peter," I tried again, "what kinds of things do you like to do? I mean, I love to go to museums and just spend time around all that good, rich art that's lasted for centuries. I love sitting in front of it and seeing it from every angle. You can learn a lot about yourself that way."

"I kind of like to hang out," Peter said.

I took another approach. I said, "I'm definitely into gourmet food because my mother's a chef and all, and I like to photograph just about anything that speaks to me about life. I try to photograph things that mean something to me, because that's kind of how I see the world, through my camera." I left lots of space here for him to jump in and say he'd love to see my work.

He didn't.

I said that *art* was the door we open to understand ourselves. I said that *artists,* like debaters and athletes, have certain depth that other people can't see. Peter fixed his ice-green eyes on me and motioned me to sit on his lap. I did, because there's more to life than sparkling conversation. He looked at me sincerely, like a dog about to be fed. I tried again.

"Peter, I've always felt that when two people really care about each other, one of the most important things they can do together is to——"

"Make dolly wet!" Marcie shouted.

I threw up my hands.

Marcie shook the doll at me. I stormed into the bathroom and filled it full.

"Go to it, kid."

She ran back to her potty chair. I shuddered. Here was a child who would never be able to sit through *The Wizard of Oz* without having to go to the bathroom.

I had hardly lunged back into the living room when Jonathan pirouetted down unannounced, and did a three-point turn on Peter's left shoulder.

"Good evening," Jonathan chirped.

He circled Peter, looking him up and down like a internist. He felt his forehead, he tapped his chin. I shot Jonathan a Supremely Irritated Look from the corner of my eye. You have to be massively subtle to pull off invisible relationships.

Peter caught it. "What's wrong?" he asked.

"Nothing . . ."

Jonathan flew toward me, his wings beating in a blur. "I must tell you, my friend, that I do not like what I see."

"Then do something, please!" I cried.

"Do w..... Peter asked.

I shouted that ..... ln't know.

Peter said he'd do *any...* for me. His eyes glazed with blind love. He gripped my ha....

Jonathan said he would think about the dilemma. Marcie announced that it was time, once again, to "make dolly wet!" I yanked the doll's head off and poured my can of 7-Up inside. Jonathan did a slow, ponderous spiral and spun backward out the window as the sounds of "Somewhere Over the Rainbow" wafted through the living room.

It was past midnight; I couldn't sleep.

I was eating a meat-loaf sandwich in my room, trying to picture what it had been like when Peter saw my face in his meat loaf and knew I was the one. I took a huge bite of sandwich. My mother made the best meat loaf in the world—dense, smoky, shouting with authority.

I had shouted for Jonathan twice since Peter drove me home. He hadn't answered. He was probably lounging on Uranus, contemplating whatever minuscule thing was wrong with *my* boyfriend.

I played the messages back on the answering machine. Pearly wanted to do an in-depth blurb on me for the Valentine edition and wanted to know where Peter and I liked to hang out and what our favorite foods were. Melissa Pageant invited me t~~~~ ~~~~birthday party. I played that one back three ~~~~es. Trish had left two messages. The first on~~~~ ~~~~d she'd asked Tucker to the dance—he said ~~~~ nated to dance, but would go with her anyw~~~~. The second one asked if I'd had any further "incidents." This depended on who you talked to.

I was really glad for Trish—she was going to the dance with someone mysterious who could benefit from in-depth psychoanalysis.

I sat on the floor of my bedroom and looked at my strapless red formal that I was going to look smashing in because the deep red offset my dark hair and made me look fiery, which is a good look for Valentine's Day, all things considered.

I dangled my drop rhinestone earrings in the eerie glow of my halogen lamp. I felt the smooth container of my Ruby Rapture lipstick. I stuffed pink Kleenex and my extra nose inhaler into my sequined evening bag. I walked to the framed eight-by-ten photo hanging on my wall that my father had taken. It was a color shot of a cardinal on an evergreen branch eating from a home-made bird feeder. Dad had taken it the Saturday of last year's King of Hearts Dance, two days after Robbie Oldsberg dumped me. Dad had wakened me up early that morning and we had driven to the country with our cameras. We'd trounced through snow-ladened forests, we'd crossed icy streams, not once talking about Robbie or Valentine's Day or my heavy, broken heart, but everything we did that day lightened me. Dad spooned peanut butter in a grapefruit rind and hung it by a pine tree for the birds to find. Two cardinals came and ate their fill. Dad and I blasted off a roll of film each through our zoom lenses. The birds flew away when I moved too close. We headed back home talking about light meters and color film, still yakking when we picked Mom up from work and went out for barbecue. Mom was asleep by ten, but Dad and I pushed through until two in the morning, watching old Marx Brothers movies and eating meat-loaf sandwiches. I knew exactly what he was doing and I loved him for it. It was the nicest day we'd ever spent together.

I touched the frame, wondering if my father would ever accept me as an artist.

Peter hadn't seemed too keen about my art either. That hurt. Todd Kovich had never understood about my work. I'd had to drag him into my studio and force him to look. I could do that with Peter, of course; he would follow me anywhere.

I wanted him to care about my art without being pushed.

I wanted us to have a decent conversation.

I needed to talk to Jonathan. There must be something he could do. Peter was just in a sensitive stage of succumbing adjustment. I'd ask him for a teensy-weensy cupid alteration. How hard could that be?

CHAPTER ELEVEN

Peter drove me to school Thursday, a shade too fast, in my opinion. He ran two red lights and almost hit a van of St. Ignatius nuns because he simply could not keep his eyes on the road for all the looking he was doing at me. At the intersection of Crosstown and Bernice I was shrieking, *"Watch the road!"* as he beamed at me like a thousand Christmas lights, screeched into the Ben Franklin parking lot, and rammed the Jeep to a sharp stop, causing the glove compartment to flop open and scores of parking tickets to flutter to the floor.

I stared at them in shock. "Peter, are these your tickets?"

He smiled and shrugged.

"You could get in trouble for not paying these!"

He scooped up the evidence. "My dad knows a guy who takes care of it." Then he pulled me close and kissed me with unbridled emotion. It would have been a much better kiss if he'd paid the tickets.

At school we were mobbed.

We were asked to be on the Prom Committee and the Graduation Committee. We were asked to join the Young Republicans, the Young Democrats, the Young Independents, and the Young Undecideds. We were asked to suggest a gift for the senior class to give to the school at graduation. I proposed a cappuccino machine for the teachers' lounge and received thunderous applause from the English Department. Deenie Wilcox asked if I would head a student panel discussing the Realities of Teenage Dating. The Student Council asked to display *my* photographs (no fewer than twelve) in the Student Center. This was the ultimate popularity nod. I was giddy with the thought.

"It will be my first private show!" I explained to Peter, who said "Uh-huh" and brushed a strand of hair from my cheek just like Todd Kovich used to do when the subject of my art came up.

"I need you to care about my work, Peter! This is what I plan to do for a living!"

He pulled me close. The hair on my arms tingled. "I care about *you*," he whispered breathlessly.

You could hardly see my locker for the forest of notes taped to it about all the upcoming parties and important in-crowd gatherings. People came at us waving appointment books, trying to fit themselves into our blockbuster schedules. I was writing dates in textbooks, on Kleenex.

I was a megatrend in the making.

I was passing old friends at a distance because the new ones kept crashing in. Trish tucked a note in my fist saying to meet by the World Peace Bench after fourth period—we had to talk. I was trying to figure out which of my photographs should grace the walls of the Student Center when Pearly Shoemaker ran up to me, her eyes twinkling like Hollywood.

"I can't tell you what it is, A.J., I swore I wouldn't talk. But when you see it, well . . . it is the absolute ultimate expression!"

"What are you talking about, Pearly?"

"You'll see." She giggled, dancing off.

I forgot about meeting Trish at fourth period. I forgot about helping Nina Bloomfeld with her Art History paper. I almost forgot to vote for that lucky macho male who would be Ben Franklin High's King of Hearts. I cast my vote (for Peter, of course). The King of

Hearts Dance Committee carried the hermetically sealed king-sized mayonnaise jars off to a soundproof, windowless room to tally the figures and swear a blood oath not to divulge the findings to *anyone* until Saturday night.

The mantle of royalty hovered above Peter's dazzling head.

At fourth period Peter taped a flower to my locker. At lunch he gave me a box of designer chocolates in the cafeteria, right by Lisa Shooty, who flamed with envy. He said, "Sweets for the sweet," which was really corny and I wished he hadn't said anything because I thought about the reams of unpaid parking tickets and cleared two rows of buttercreams in under three minutes. At sixth period he gave me a silver bracelet. At seventh period he gave me his school jacket, at eighth period he tried to give me money.

"Just pick out a little something nice for yourself. . . ," he explained.

Gifts were always appropriate, but cash seemed tacky. I refused the money.

It happened during ninth period.

Peter had just handed me his watch as a supreme token of affection, when I said, "We need to talk about things, Peter; *communicate* . . ."

Peter said, fine, whatever I wanted. I said I wanted a conversation, and he said, okay, whatever I wanted. We sat there at Big Ben's feet for a while and didn't say anything. We walked around and didn't say anything.

"I wonder why we never went out before?" he asked.

I looked down and shrugged. There were probably *lots* of disconnected reasons. Our lockers were on different floors; he was in love with Julia Hart.

His gorgeous face hardened. "I wasn't attracted to you," he sneered. "I thought you were weird!"

"Oh?"

"Yeah," he continued, "I tend to go for knockout blondes. You don't exactly qualify." He put his arm around me. "I'm not into girls who search for meaning . . ."

"Really?"

He shook his head, laughing. "I like girls who . . ." He was giving me an extremely lecherous look here when his eyes blurred, his cheeks went pale. He shook his head. "What was I doing?"

I moved away. "You were being a jerk."

Peter rubbed his temple. "I'm sorry, I . . ." He walked toward me, arms outstretched, devotion, once again, carved into his face. He reached desperately for me, our eyes met. His were dull, lifeless.

I backed off.

He said we could do our homework together; I said homework was something you did alone in extreme agony, not something you shared with another individual.

Peter said we could have dinner together; I said I wasn't hungry. I said maybe I should just walk home from school today—we didn't have to do every single thing together. He said he'd just drive down the street slowly to make sure I was safe.

He drove me home. Stieglitz went berserk when he walked me to the porch. He hugged me good-bye like I was leaving for a two-year stint with the Peace Corps. I ran into the house, locked all three dead bolts, and turned around to hear a mythological whoosh heralding Jonathan, just in from never-never land.

"Your hands," he observed, "are shaking."

So were my legs and a portion of my chest cavity.

"I would listen to my instincts if I were you, my friend."

My heart was thumping too hard to hear anything.

"You must look to the core of what you believe and act accordingly," said Jonathan. "You must listen to the things that you try to ignore."

I leaned against the front door and started to cry.

It was Friday morning. I was going for the world record in Sleepless, Comatose Living While Attempting to Finish Senior Year. Mom had left hours before. We passed in the hall like ships in the night. She asked why I was still up and I said I'd forgotten how to sleep. She patted my arm and said eventually I'd remember.

I was tiptoeing out the back door to drive myself to school when Peter screeched up the driveway in his Jeep. He handed me a thermos of hot chocolate and a large stuffed bear that was certain to terrify Stieglitz and said I would never need my car again. *He* would take me everywhere.

"I like my car . . ."

I looked longingly at my almost classic sixteen-year-old Volvo wasting away in the garage as Peter buckled my safety belt for me. It would always be like this, he promised. I was beginning to believe him.

When we got to school, Pearly Shoemaker was wailing like a mourner in the Student Center because the truck with the Valentine edition had not arrived. Her cheeks were hot pink, her temples were pounding.

"The truck," she shrieked, "was due here at seven-fifteen, it is now eight oh-one—the truck, A.J., loaded with vision and promise and prepaid advertisements!"

She flailed her arms toward me. "It could have been hijacked by psychotic fiends! St. Ignatius would do something that despicable!"

I leaned against a fake marble pillar and sighed with deep meaning. "Their nuns would kill them, Pearly."

She slumped off.

I gazed up at the tall, kindly figure of Benjamin Franklin, who had commanded respect through honesty, as Trish Beckman pounced on me like Catwoman.

"How long have we been friends?" she demanded,

touching Tucker's SAVE THE WHALES pin like it was a diamond.

Guilt gripped me. "Seven years, Trish." I saw no point in lying.

"During which time we have told each other everything, we have always been completely honest!"

This was almost true. I had held back a few times, like when she got her hair cut last year and I said she looked great even though she looked like a deranged elf. I gulped.

"I sat with you, A.J., when you were blocked on your photography for three solid months. You sat with me when Bob Sarento went out with that exchange student from France." I did too. "I cried for—"

"Two grading periods," I interjected.

"Three," she said. *"What is going on? Peter Terris is a roboton; he just lurches through the halls looking for you. He flunked his Public Speaking test! He was supposed to talk for three minutes on World Peace and all he said was that Ghandi had the right idea, and then he sat down! And you,"* Trish continued, "you look positively hunted! I'm not leaving until you tell me everything!"

I so need to tell you, Trish . . .

The bell rang for fifth period. Trish blocked my path. "Bells don't matter, A.J.!"

Friendship matters, I wailed inside. *I'm a wretched friend!*

Jonathan slinked down from the ceiling, waxing

his bow like grinding emotional trauma was all part of the rich pageant of life.

"Tell her," said Jonathan, "that you have had an experience that you cannot explain."

Tell me about it.

I choked on my tongue, but pushed the words out.

"What kind of experience?" Trish demanded.

Jonathan fluttered his wings; my mind cleared. "Do you remember the time you slept over at my house and we were looking out my bedroom window and we saw that little flash in the sky that nobody else saw and then we felt like an entire civilization was watching us?"

"Yeah . . . ?"

"Weirder than that."

Trish considered this. That night had been a total, emotional blowout that we still talked about sometimes, but only late at night to get the full, freaky impact. She shuddered. "Have you seen something?" she asked.

"More or less . . ."

"Did Peter see it too?"

At that moment Peter appeared at my side, grabbed my hand, and whispered "I love you" in my ear, loud enough for Trish to hear. She grabbed her heart and stepped back.

Jonathan fluttered his wings in her direction and she said she had to go, just as chirpy as you please. She turned and skipped off to her drama class, where she was cast as Stella in Scene One of *A Streetcar Named Desire* opposite Billy Bunting, who, in my opinion, couldn't get anyone worked up about anything. I had study hall this period, which seemed inanely insignificant, now that Peter Terris had just said the *L* word in front of my best friend.

He cuddled close and gave me the full force of his ice-green eyes that were clouded with cupid manipulation. "I love you!" he repeated rather loudly, like a person expounding a great, freeing truth.

I couldn't speak.

Peter grinned at me like a goon. "I will always love you!" he shouted as several students looked in our direction in massive shock. *"Always!"* he shouted even louder.

I yanked him behind the sainted statue of Big Ben. *"Peter!* Just calm down. I am into subtlety in relationships. We don't want the whole world to know."

I glared at Jonathan, who was buzzing around wearing his internist's expression, *doing nothing*! He examined his dinky arrows, he whistled, he landed on top of Big Ben's hat and twirled like a top as Peter Terris jumped up on Ben's bronze base and declared, "I want the whole world to know that *I love A. J. McCreary!*"

My face burned with humiliation. *"Stop it, Peter!"*

Peter said, "I love it when you get fiery," and took my hand.

I took it back.

I looked at his deeply gorgeous face. *What have I done?*

"It's heeeeeeeere, boys and girls!" shouted Pearly Shoemaker, running up to us holding a stack of thick Valentine *Oracle*s. "The truck driver got lost! Can you believe who they let drive trucks these days?"

Peter grabbed an *Oracle* and held it over his head like it was a trophy. "Hey, everybody!" he shouted, *"I'm in love!"*

My brain clogged.

Pearly dropped the newspapers in a free fall. Bobby Pershing stopped ogling girls. Melissa Pageant stopped brazenly flirting with Tony Denko. Lisa Shooty stopped bouncing. Julia Hart spun around like she'd been pinched from behind. A teeming mass of Ben Franklin students froze in unbelief as the impact of Peter's words hung in the Student Center like passed gas.

I closed my eyes because I could not cope with unbridled devotion. An oppressive, twisting ooze wound its way around my neck as Peter Terris, the most popular boy in school, gazed into my eyes like a universal, card-carrying dip.

I needed fresh air.

I lunged toward the door and pushed it open as the cold streams of February gusts slapped my face. I sucked in freezing oxygen.

Peter picked me up from behind and twirled me around.

"This is not a good time for me, Peter"—I grabbed my throat—"I'm getting strep throat, I think, and—"

"Everybody thinks its cool not to show you care . . ." He did a jump and twist like a circus performer. "I think that's stupid."

"I think, Peter, that there's a lot to say for consummate denial!"

Bobby Pershing leaned against the trophy case. Jessica Wong dropped her book bag and didn't pick it up. Nina Bloomfeld crashed to her knees in the middle of the Student Center. Peter's face broke into pure, unfiltered sunshine. "I've found the best girl in the world and I don't care who knows it!"

I was mortified. That's when Dr. Strictland, Principal from Purgatory, stampeded onto the scene.

"Young man," she shouted, "*what* are you doing?"

"I'm expressing my love!" Peter shouted. I lowered my head, appalled.

"And just where, young man, is your fifth-period class?"

Peter said he didn't remember, he was so worked up. He said he didn't even care, because when you've come face to face with the real thing, fifth period doesn't matter. Not caring about fifth period really got Dr. Strictland going.

"High school, young man, is no place to express your love for whoever it is . . . !"

Peter beamed and pointed at me. "It's *her*!" he declared. "Isn't she *wonderful*?"

Dr. Strictland peered at me, unbelieving.

I coughed and waved and flounced back my hair to appear to be someone worthy of ecstatic devotion. My glory escaped her. Jonathan did a backflip in front of Dr. Strictland's face, which had changed from tombstone gray into serious scarlet because Peter was singing me a love song, for crying out loud, a lame, pathetic love song in front of half the school.

"I love youuuuuuuuuu!" he crooned.

I shut my eyes in supreme agony.

"Open them, my friend," ordered Jonathan. "Observe the fulfillment of your wish."

CHAPTER TWELVE

I said "Excuse me" to Dr. Strictland, who was eyeing me, thunderstruck. I needed to step outside for a moment to collect myself, possibly puke. She stepped aside as I tore out the door with Jonathan. No principal, dead or alive, will deny a puking request.

I ran until I couldn't run anymore. I slumped against Bobby Pershing's old Buick in the school parking lot and lurched toward Jonathan with massive intensity.

"Do something, Jonathan! Shoot him, sprinkle him, make him *normal*! *Please*!"

Jonathan straightened his dinky pink sash. "I am afraid, my friend, that adjustments are not within my realm of influence."

"What do you mean?"

"I mean," Jonathan explained firmly, "that you have your wish—a living, breathing, totally smitten boyfriend."

"But he's not going to stay like this forever, right?"

Jonathan began packing up his dinky quiver.

"He's going to snap out of it, right?"

"My work is finished," Jonathan said. "I must leave you."

Coldness swept through my soul.

"But . . . you can't. . . ," I stammered, "I can't . . . live with this!"

"It is most unfortunate, my friend."

"Jonathan, I need you to help me! We're a team, right? *Friends?*" I reached out for him; he zipped out of the way.

He looked at me through pained eyes. "It is not my place to repair anything, my friend. It is your responsibility to live with the consequences of your decision."

"But what am I going to do?"

A small tear rolled down Jonathan's cheek. "This

is always," he whispered, "the most painful part of the Visitation. I truly wish you well, Allison Jean McCreary."

I stared at him, unbelieving.

Jonathan put the last of his arrows in his quiver, lowered his head, and pushed off into the air like a proud, graceful bird.

"Jonathan!"

I leapt up to grab him, to hold him and make him stay, but it was too late. I shouted that I wasn't looking for the world here, just a few minor personality adjustments!

I flailed at the air. *"You can't leave me now!"*

But he did.

His tiny wings sped to a blur. Jonathan Livingston Cupid soared above the locust trees, zoomed through a cloud, and was history.

It was a full-page ad, that's the first thing you noticed about it. It had singing cupids and happy hearts and flying birds with petals in their beaks. It said, PETER TERRIS LOVES A.J. MCCREARY FOREVER in enormous letters—the FOREVER was in script to give it more foreverness. It lay there on page twenty-three of the *Oracle* Valentine edition like dog doo on a newly mowed lawn. It was directly across from Tucker Crawford's article on being alone, which should give Tucker an eternal yuk. Pearly

Shoemaker said it had cost Peter megabucks to run it. Never in all her years of high-school journalism had she seen such adoration. Pearly couldn't believe I hadn't laid eyes on the ad until now, since the whole school had and was talking about nothing else. Pearly said the *Oracle* was a premier hit—everyone had bought a copy, everyone was overcome by my searing cover shot, everyone said that like Donna, deep down they were wholly, unalterably *confused.*

Pearly placed a well-manicured nail on my book bag. "You have spoken to your generation, A.J. And in the very same issue you have captured what every female dreams of seeing—total devotion in print!"

I folded the total devotion so I wouldn't have to look at it.

"Of course," she continued, "I think your finest work has been for the paper, A.J. I can see your entire photography exhibit in the Student Center glorifying your grandest *Oracle* moments."

I said I couldn't think about that now.

"Don't forget the Science Week cover shot, A.J., of Rodney Harris covered with frog carcasses. That's one of my favorites."

I stood at my locker wearing a ski cap and dark glasses. I was hoping I would not be recognized, hoping I could make it to English Lit without Peter organizing a twenty-one-gun salute and a Rose Bowl parade in my honor.

"There you are!" Peter cried, sneaking up from behind.

I pulled my ski cap over my eyes.

"I've been so worried," he blurted out. "I couldn't find you . . ."

"I'm here!" I shrieked. *"I'm fine!"*

He walked me to English Lit; he swept me to Art History. Peter Terris was everywhere I looked. I tried to ignore him—this was tough, since he was six four. I kept hoping he'd pull out of it; I kept praying this was just a passing squall.

His eyes got foggier.

His voice got louder.

His stare got creepier.

"Don't you blink?" I shrieked. *"Your eyeballs could dry up! You could be blind before we graduate!"*

"I think you're beautiful, A.J.!" Peter shouted, looking pathetic.

It was all my fault.

I buried my head in my sleeve so he couldn't hear my muffled "Aaaaarrrrgggggg!" as three sophomore girls walked by with cameras slung over their shoulders.

I looked at Big Ben, who had done so much for America by being stalwart and saying what he felt no matter what the consequences, who now held a large red

Valentine in his hand with a grinning, potbellied cupid, courtesy of the King of Hearts Dance Committee.

Was no American, dead or alive, immune from this holiday?

I was slumped in the family room, curled into the fetal position on the old corduroy couch, where I could get good and depressed better than anywhere. My body sagged. I was a monster. A total beast. I had turned Peter into a lovesick bore and he would never, ever be free from my extreme charms.

Stieglitz licked my hand as terror swept through my soul.

Jonathan would *not* up and leave me in a potential nightmare!

Would he?

Then a jolt of clear-eyed reality hit me.

I shot straight up.

"Wait a minute!" I shouted, *"Magic is never one-sided!"*

Stieglitz barked in agreement.

There was *always* a way to weasel out; everyone knew that. True, it was usually a weird way, like giving your firstborn child to a gnarled dwarf, but heroines under stress promise all kinds of things.

Alice got out of Wonderland, didn't she?

Sleeping Beauty woke up.

I wouldn't give up without a fight!

I had to find Jonathan!

I threw on my black bomber jacket as Stieglitz, trusty canine sidekick, leapt to my side.

"Find Jonathan, boy!"

Stieglitz sat down, confused.

"Stieglitz, this is life and death!"

Stieglitz lay down and hid his head.

"Oh, never mind!"

I checked the house first, since cupids were sneaky and into concealment. I looked in closets, coat pockets, I checked behind the couch, under the chair cushions.

"Jonathan," I said sweetly, "I'm not angry anymore, little guy. You can come out now. *You've made your point!"*

I checked Jonathan's favorite places—the ceiling fan, my bookcase. "Ally, ally oxen free!" I cried.

No cupid.

I searched my studio, ransacked my bedroom.

"Jonathan," I crooned, "I will be delighted to work with you now. We can be a happy, productive team!"

I charged outside with Stieglitz. I peered behind trees and whistled. I shook bare winter bushes as Mrs. Borderbuck, our next-door neighbor, watched me suspiciously from her kitchen window.

"Jonathan," I chirped, "where are you?"

My ears strained for the sound of cupid wings.

I flung the garage door up and jumped into the

Volvo. "Okay, Jonathan! Then we start at the beginning!"

I rammed the Volvo into first gear and sped to the Nickleby Novelty Company, where the nightmare had begun.

"May I help you, hon?" asked the receptionist at the Nickleby Novelty Company, popping her gum. Behind her desk was a wall display of Nickleby's products: whoopee cushions, disappearing candles, rubber bugs, all the necessities of the fun life.

"I'm looking for a cupid," I said in my best *Dragnet* voice.

"Yeah, sweetie"—she rolled her eyes—"aren't we all?"

"A used cupid," I said.

"Everything's new here, doll," she explained, looking behind her. "The only cupid we got's that one." She pointed to a pink rubber cupid. "You put water in it," she explained. "It squirts out there." She made a face. "Some people, huh?"

"He was stuffed, ma'am. He rolled out of one of your boxes."

She eyed me strangely. "Haven't ever seen a stuffed one here," she said, "and I been here thirteen years. We got stuffed angels though." She held a puffy angel up and pressed its stomach; it burped. "We got stuffed lips and stuffed snakes; that's it. We're getting out of stuffed and doing more rubber."

"That's wise," I said, backing out the door.

I drove to the Crestport Beach and checked the Snack Shack for arrow pricks; it was clean. I stood on the DONNA IS CONFUSED rock and held up a sign that read CAN WE TALK?

I crashed to my knees on the cold, icy beach: "Jonathan. . . ," I cried, *"I need you!"*

I checked the answering machine back home; Jonathan hadn't called.

I left my parents a note saying that I was grappling with the bleak vicissitudes of life, I would not be home for dinner, and that they shouldn't worry. I then did the only thing left for a thinking teenager to do: I squared my shoulders and hit the mall.

I stormed through every store that could carry cupids. Sold out, I was told.

"They were here last week!" I screeched at a poor salesperson. "Glaring at people with little beady eyes!" The salesperson shrugged and said maybe cupids were becoming a craze.

"God help us," I said.

I bought fifteen Valentines with cupids on them, hid in a stall in the women's lounge, and attempted contact.

"All right," I snarled, glaring at each dumpy illustration, *"which one of you guys knows Jonathan?"*

They were silent, but I wasn't fooled. They were listening.

I snarled. *"Just tell Jonathan that A. J. McCreary's in town and I'm looking for him!"*

I burst from the stall to find a woman and small child staring at me like I was naked.

"Don't look at her, Ashley!" the woman demanded.

Ashley covered her face and was swept to safety; the woman looked over her shoulder to make sure I hadn't grown neck hair. I checked myself in the mirror; nothing mangy had happened. Yet.

I bought a ten-dollar white chocolate cupid at Camille's Confections: *"Talk to me!"* I shrieked at it.

The cupid said nothing. I tried to return it, since ten bucks is ten bucks.

"He's not what I expected," I said to the confection woman.

Her eyebrows shot up. "What were you expecting?"

"More personality," I mumbled.

She looked at me like a shrink watches a psycho. "Candy's not returnable, miss."

"Or cooperative," I said, snarling, and ate the cupid's white chocolate head in grief.

I went to the library and pored through second-rate cupid literature looking for clues. There was nothing on how to contact one. They just showed up, like wasps.

I drove home, dejected. If you can't find an answer at the mall or the library, what does that say about the world? I pulled into the garage; the automatic door locked behind me with grim finality.

CHAPTER THIRTEEN

I chewed my thumbnail as dawn sneaked across the sky, and braced myself for another fun day in the Magic Kingdom.

It was Valentine's Day.

My cupid was at large.

I spent the morning toiling at the Emotional Gourmet, selling dinky heart-shaped cheesecakes that my mother was afraid wouldn't sell because they were too cute. They flew off the shelves—as Sonia says, "There's no such thing as too cute on Valentine's Day."

The shop was thick with Valentine madness. Lobster salad twinkled in crystal bowls, candied apple slices peeked from every corner. Chocolate truffle cakes beckoned from heart-shaped trays. Shiny hearts and thick lace hung from doors and display cases. Happy, loving couples lined the counters, oohing and ahhhing at the breadth of gastronomic glory before them. The whole world was in love.

Except me.

I ladled bouillabaisse into containers and tried to remember the exact moment of death.

Was it when Peter asked why we'd never gone out before?

Was it when the parking tickets fell on the car floor?

Was it when he shouted the *L* word in the Student Center instead of the backseat of a Chevy, where it would have been appropriate and expected?

I reached for the good memories to crowd out the bad—the looks, the feelings, the smiles, the embraces that had fed my soul for those whirlwind days. I could still see them, but they were out of focus. I wondered if it was possible for Peter and me to be a happy, cooing couple again. He appeared at that moment, swooshed through the doors of the Emotional Gourmet, like a knight returning from the Crusades to seek his fair maiden. It was all I could do to keep my breakfast down.

"*A.J.!!*" he cried dreamily.

"Yo," I said back.

He gave me a bouquet of white roses and said he loved me, he lugged a Valentine the size of a Ford Taurus up to the counter and said I was his entire world. He followed me as I ran screaming into the kitchen, handed me a box of Valentine candy, and was about to start singing when I went for aggressive action, shoved two *biscotti* in his mouth, and pushed him against the deep freeze.

"Don't," I threatened, "*sing*! Don't say *anything* personal!"

Peter made a slight gagging sound and nodded.

"I don't like it when you shout your feelings about me in front of other people! I don't want you to do it anymore! Do we understand one another?"

Peter mumbled something through the *biscotti*. I sat him down like Henry Higgins did with Eliza Doolittle and tried to point out the subtleties of a caring, responsible teen relationship. I did this because *nothing* was going to make me miss this dance. I had clawed my way to get here and I wasn't backing out.

"Let's take it from the top," I instructed, "no shrieking your love . . ."

Peter nodded.

"No panting . . ."

"Is groaning all right, A.J.?"

"Don't push my buttons, Peter."

Orlando, the assistant chef, glared at me, disgusted. I deserved it.

"It's not what you think, Orlando, and don't tell my mother."

"Don't tell your mother what?" Mom appeared from the basement holding a salami.

"Nothing," I said as Orlando punched a mound of brioche dough for men's rights. "Ha ha," I added, and slinked back on the floor as Trish Beckman, Psychologist-in-Training, entered the store in a bold sweep, wearing an expression that can best be described as inflamed.

"I would like," Trish said hotly, "six lemon custard muffins and to know the *real* reason why you are destroying your life and our friendship."

Now at this point I was a person who was going on maybe five hours of sleep over the last three days. This is not enough rest in which to search your heart for the law of kindness.

I rankled. *"Just cap it, Trish! I don't need the heat. I don't need the condemnation!"*

She leaned toward me, her eyes on fire. "And what do you need, A.J.?"

"To be alone!"

"Take a break, hon, will you?" begged Sonia.

I pushed through the kitchen with Trish at my heels, past Peter, who had swallowed the *biscotti* and now cried out, "There you are!" I opened the first door I saw and stormed right in. It was the walk-in refrigerator. I was alone—and freezing.

I stood there feeling inane, surrounded by dairy products and cholesterol-laden meats. The door opened and Trish crashed inside.

"So," she said looking around strangely, "it's come to this."

I said it sure had.

"I've left messages, A.J. You haven't bothered to return one!"

"I'm having a really rough time!"

"You didn't meet me during fourth period!"

"I forgot. I'm sorry."

"You look awful!"

I felt worse. I said I needed to keep what bleak emotional reserves I had for the dance. I said things with Peter were more complicated than I'd figured. I said I was really glad about her and Tucker—I wanted to know *everything*—I just needed to get through today without crumbling, at which point I would go back to being a supremely committed friend, but the sheer act of survival was going to take every ounce of strength I had. I handed her a piece of prosciutto as a peace offering.

She refused it. "I don't know what's going on with Peter Terris, why he's acting the way he is, but I can tell you that it's not healthy. Every feeling he has been distorted."

I hung my head in shame; I felt so lonely. Icicles were forming on my nostrils. Trish didn't care. "There are plenty of girls at school who would kill to be in your position, A.J. They think you've struck a blow for females everywhere. But I wouldn't, because the whole thing has changed you. You're so caught up in the in-crowd number that you've forgotten about your friends and who you are. You don't carry your camera anymore, you don't even smile. Peter Terris is all gaga over you and you are positively miserable!"

Tears stung my eyes.

"If this is what you call love, A.J., I don't want any part of it!"

And with that Trish Beckman, best friend through thick and thin, stormed out of the walk-in refrigerator in the ultimate theatrical exit and left me alone to lean against a box of Canadian bacon and contemplate my thrill-packed future with Peter Terris, the human equivalent of Super Glue.

I was sitting in my Volvo outside the driveway of the Ben Franklin Student Center watching the student workers carry in the big Bose speakers for the extravaganza rock and roll group Heather and the Heartbeats, who would be performing live for us tonight. Gary Quark's brother was dating one of the Heartbeats who sang the doo-wop parts and the group gave Ben Franklin High a significant discount on the price. Gary said it also helped that they hadn't had a booking since October.

Joel Winger carried in a big red carpet. Chloe Bittleman lugged in trays of food. The sun set, leaving harsh, spindly shadows, giving the school a state-penitentiary flair.

I shuddered and flashed my brights. Maybe Jonathan would see my SOS and respond. I rolled down my window. "Jonathan," I whispered, "please come back."

But there was nothing.

I curled into a half ball. I wanted to be in love again. I wanted to be dying to see Peter instead of recoiling at the thought. I drew a broken heart on the frost of my windshield and sniffed. No one wants to be between engagements.

But the show must go on.

I sat up and slammed the Volvo into first. I had to make the best of a snaky situation.

I would embrace the King of Hearts Dance like my father had embraced advertising. I would stick it in everybody's face who had ever broken up with me and look positively smashing, although the smashing part would only happen if I got a nap. I would be remembered by my classmates as the girl who brought Peter Terris to his knees.

I said, "Jonathan, if you're listening. . . ," and then I stopped. I knew he wasn't.

I steered the Volvo out of the parking lot and headed home to become dazzling.

I was sitting at the kitchen table in my bathrobe, waiting for my nails to dry, waiting for the hot curlers in my hair to work a miracle on my dark, mysterious tresses that had given up around five this afternoon along with my skin and the rest of my body. Stieglitz had diarrhea. He whined pathetically, which meant he had to go outside *again.* I opened the back door for him and said that life was tough, but to be grateful he was a dog. Being human was brutal.

I sighed deeply. I needed one thing to go right today.

Dad padded into the kitchen, holding the *Oracle* Valentine edition.

"Your mother," he began uncertainly, "left this on my . . ."

He cleared his throat and looked down, pained.

"What I'm trying to say, A.J., is that this shot is very good. It's got humor, symmetry, light balance . . ."

I brightened.

"It's the best work you've done," he added. "I mean it."

I was positively beaming. "That means so much, Dad."

I should have just basked in the glow, but I so needed to hear more.

I touched his arm. "Do you think I could make it with my art, Dad? Do you think I have enough talent?"

He was quiet for a long time. His eyes narrowed. His shoulders sagged.

"I'm not disputing you have real talent, A.J, but talent and making it in the art world do not go hand in hand. Do you know how many photographers there are in this world with real talent who can't even scratch out a living?"

At that moment I wanted another father. I stood up, shaking. "What if I'm one of the thousands who can make it, Dad? What if I'm good enough and I *don't even try?*"

I grabbed the *Oracle* Valentine edition, raced past him, and pounded up the stairs.

I took out my curlers and brushed my hair upside down in epic frustration with Mom's megabrush to add extra fullness; I got limpness instead. I picked up a droopy strand of brown hair and watched it freefall across my sunken face. Peter was due in fifteen minutes. I looked dead.

Mom appeared at my door and studied me like I was a pie in the oven with a faulty crust. "Into the bathroom!" she ordered.

I went glumly.

"Put your head down," she directed.

Mom grabbed the megabrush and said I needed to listen to her. She started brushing my hair in flowing movements like she was whipping cream.

"I've known your father for twenty-two years, A.J., and I can tell you that he would do just about anything to spare you the pain he experienced as a filmmaker."

"Great . . ."

She sprayed mousse through my scalp, lifting and fluffing and coaxing my hair to behave.

"He's swimming from a long way off on this one, honey. It's not fair, but it's where he is right now. Shake out your hair."

I shook.

She ran cold water in the tub.

"Stick your feet in."

"It's freezing, Mom, I'll—"

"This," Mom declared, "can wake the dead. Tonight you qualify."

I stuck my feet in arctic water and was hurled into an energizing rush of consciousness. Mom turned to examine my face. She yanked out the heavy artillery, her middle-aged eye-care kit. It must be bad.

"Look up," she ordered, and went to town.

She covered me and decorated me like a poor, cracked cake that had to be rescued for company. She put a light covering of mascara on my eyes, powdered my cheeks with pink, glowing blush. She said, "We all have old ghosts we have to fight. Your dad is arm-wrestling with his right now. Can you live with that?"

I fidgeted.

Mom looked at me with exhausted eyes. "Can you at least try?"

I sniffed and said I guess I could.

"Is Dad going to be okay?"

"Eventually," she said. "In the meantime a little compassion wouldn't hurt."

I nodded.

Mom stepped back, satisfied, and turned me toward the mirror.

"The natural look," she announced. "It takes a lot longer, but it's worth it."

I stood before the bathroom mirror, a teenager reborn. My hair hung lush, layered, and full. Underneath it was ratted and sprayed to high heaven—but no one would be looking there. Everything tonight was on the surface. My face shone with a deep pink glow, my eye angst had been obliterated. I put on Ruby Rapture lipstick and blotted my lips in the perfect outline of a kiss.

Mom pushed me back into the bedroom, tossed me my killer red dress, my sequined shoes. In minutes I stood before my full-length antique mirror, having achieved smashing.

The doorbell reverberated in my ear. Stieglitz looked at me mournfully and didn't bark.

I turned to Mom—our eyes locked in one of those

parent / child moments people talk about when they're old. I ran to get the door before Dad, in case Peter started yodeling or something lame. I'd make my big entrance at the dance.

Ta da.

Dad beat me to the door. Peter greeted him with an enthusiasm only seen among used-car salesmen. *"Mr. McCreary!"* he began.

I crashed between them. "I'm ready!"

Dad's face turned soft when he saw me. He squeezed my hand with massive depth. I squeezed his back with consummate compassion.

"Well. . . ," Dad said, beaming.

I took a deep breath.

Peter stammered that I was beautiful.

Mom admired her handiwork.

I did a little twirl and grinned.

Peter looked fabulous—it's amazing what a tux can do for a bozo. He was holding a red-and-white rose corsage that was, without a doubt, the most gorgeous corsage I'd ever seen. He tried to pin it on me and nicked my skin. He acted as though he'd bludgeoned me, he was so upset, and Mom and Dad looked at each other strangely when he kept repeating that he would never, ever do anything to hurt me . . .

I whispered, "Don't talk," got the corsage in place, and pricked my finger.

Dad had his camera and was taking pictures of us.

It was good to see him with it again—he hadn't held a camera in ages. I really hate having my picture taken, most photographers do, but it was important to Dad, who was in heavy combat against the phantoms of the past, so I played along and posed like I was the happiest person on the planet. Mom leaned against the grandfather clock in the hall, taking it all in. I could tell she didn't buy it. Dad put his camera down and looked at me nervously, like all fathers do when their teenage daughters are dressed to kill and can pass for twenty-five-year-old women.

"Boy, those nails of yours sure are red," he muttered.

Mom tucked her arm in his to keep him still.

Peter promised my parents that he would take excellent care of me, he would never leave my side, not for a minute. When you've found the girl of your dreams, he said, the girl who fulfills your every hope and desire, you're sure not going to be a jerk and let her out of your sight. Mom and Dad listened, their smiles growing thin. Peter said he had written a poem about me and would everyone like to hear it?

I said, "Gee, this has been nice," and yanked him out the door into the waiting white stretch limo and the frozen tundra of high-school memories.

CHAPTER FOURTEEN

The limo pulled up to the front of Ben Franklin High and came to a leisurely stop to make sure everyone drinking beer in the parking lot was paying attention. A limo had never been seen at the King of Hearts Dance to my knowledge—limos were reserved for proms—but when you are impending royalty, you do these things as a matter of course.

The driver opened the door as a dutiful coachman and Peter bounded out to help me. Getting out of a car gracefully has never been my strong suit, especially in heels, and I scooted closer to the door so I wouldn't have to lunge, swung my legs around, and tottered up to victory. Peter said "Thank you, my good man" to the driver, which was really lame, but not as lame as what he did next—picking me up, that is—*carrying* me over an ice puddle so I wouldn't get my shoes wet. I was flailing my arms to break free when I heard Lisa Shooty ask Al Costanzo how come he never carried *her* over puddles? I saw Heidi Morganthaller glare at Jeff Dintsman, who apparently didn't carry her either. I told Peter he could put me down and smiled like a southern belle who had just lost the family estate and planned to keep the news to herself.

He lowered me gently like I was a rare, delicate thing. I squared my sexy shoulders, took Peter's hand, and swept inside the Student Center doors, redefining majestic.

I sucked in my breath at the sight: the Student Center had been transformed into unparalleled Valentine splendor.

Hundreds of hearts twinkled, iridescent lights shone from tables, walls, and chairs. Sparkling students floated among crepe paper and lace. Scads of red, pink, and white helium balloons decorated the stage. Giant King of Hearts playing cards surrounded the dance floor. A spiral white staircase rose directly to the left of the sainted statue of Big Ben himself, who was clad in a makeshift equivalent of Valentine boxer shorts. The banner above the stage read, WHEN TWO HEARTS BEAT AS ONE . . . Everyone looked supreme. There were more girls wearing red dresses than anything, but my dress was the reddest.

Peter took my arm and led me through the WHEN TWO HEARTS BEAT AS ONE archway that was shaped like the inside of a real heart and made lub-dub noises when Roger Dexter, president of the Electronics Club, pushed the control button and kicked the side. Peter had to duck down to get through the heart, but I didn't. It was just my size. Everything tonight was just for me!

We paraded down the royal-red carpet and stepped onto the dance floor, bathed in low, earthy light. I threw back my shoulders and tossed out my hair.

Ta da!

I pranced past Robbie Oldsberg, Connecticut's premier rodent, and his mousy date. I looked Julia Hart straight in her baby-blue eyes and she looked away first. I shouted hi to Trish as she hurried by in pink silk with Tucker, her face flushed with love. Tucker looked like he would rather be having brain surgery than be at a school dance. Trish said hi back flatly so I'd know she was still ripped.

"You look great," I muttered as she rounded the buffet table.

"*You* look great," Peter whispered to me.

A spotlight illuminated the stage. Popularity surged through my veins. Gary Quark, resplendent in a lime-green tux, announced Heather and the Heartbeats, who danced out in glittering dresses and mile-high hair. Heather asked everyone if we were ready to have a really good time.

"*Yes!*" we shouted.

Were we ready to celebrate Valentine's Day like no school had ever celebrated it before?

"*Yes!*" we hollered.

Were we ready—Heather checked the banner—to have our hearts beat as one?

"*Yes!*" we answered unequivocally.

I could feel the magic tingling in my toes. I could feel the silk of my killer red dress hugging me in all the right places. I could feel Peter's glazed eyes staring at me.

"I don't think I can keep my feelings inside," he protested.

"*Swallow them!*"

He gulped.

Heather shouted, "Let's do it!" as the big, glittering Valentine heart above the dance floor began to twirl. The band broke into pure, unadulterated rock and roll, and the boogying began.

Most guys are rotten dancers, but not Peter. We sensed each other's moves, twisted at the same pace. My skirt was twirling, my hair was flying, and most importantly, Peter wasn't talking. Rays of stardom bounced off the sequins on my killer red shoes, announcing to the world that A. J. McCreary had finally arrived!

We danced three fast dances without a break, and I wasn't even breathing hard' when Heather crooned a syrupy ballad and we fell into our partner's arms, shuffling and swaying down to slow dancing. Peter draped himself around me like a hormone-drenched gorilla and I tried to look appropriately lost in the moment. All around us love-soaked couples clutched each other in massive emoting. I wanted to be emoting too, but when you're Queen of the Hop you can't have everything.

Peter was nuzzling *very* close, making breathing difficult. He was about to whisper something grimly devoted when Heather called for a line dance. Everyone made room for Peter and me to lead. Up to the front we ran, raising our hands, shimmying down. Kids jumped in behind us unafraid, kids I'd never figured would join a line dance, but everyone was a hoofer tonight, except for Trish and Tucker. It makes you appreciate the depth of the teenage soul. It makes you realize how we're all so much more than we appear in the cafeteria. I wanted to shout that as their leader, I would not fail them. I knew what it was like to be a shadow in the Student Center and I wouldn't forget from whence I had come. I twirled the line into a unified circle symbolizing the depth of the hormonal experience that we all shared. We were churning on the downbeat, the chaperons were clapping from the sidelines, everything twirled round and round in a great rush of Valentine splendor. The line broke left and we faced the stage, clapping and shouting as the Heartbeats sang "oo wa oo" on the backup with profound meaning. Jody Barnabo was taking photographs; it was strange to be in the center of the action instead of on the sidelines photographing it. I jumped left, right, and gave her all my best expressions. That's when Peter stopped dead in his tracks, grinned at me maniacally, and shouted to the air like a supreme loon:

"Isn't she great?"

I can't describe the horror.

"I mean," he continued to the dancing crowd representing, and I'm estimating here, every person I've ever met in my bleak life, *"look at her, will you all?"*

Everyone looked.

And you know how it is when everyone's looking at you—you imagine all sorts of things. I checked my nose to make sure nothing was hanging out of it and tried to make the best of the worst moment of my life.

I mumbled that I wasn't that great.

"Oh, yes, you are!" Peter cried, picking me up against my personal will and twirling me in public.

"Oh, no, I'm not!" I said, snarling, digging my manicured nails into his neck.

Heather and the Heartbeats, capping the moment, broke into "Your Love Is Lifting Me Higher," and Peter followed suit, lifting me higher still, as the crowd cheered and I burned with humiliation, finally wriggling myself into position to let loose a debilitating kick to his shin.

He put me down.

"Never," I hissed, "do that again!"

Peter was rubbing his leg. "I'm sorry, baby, I—"

I grabbed the lapels of his tux. "I'm almost five nine, buster! I'm not anybody's *baby!*"

I stormed from the dance floor, found the closest folding chair, and crumpled into a heartrending heap. Lisa Shooty dashed to my side. *"How* did you get him to do that, A.J.?"

I searched her perfect face for signs of sarcasm. She was serious.

I looked at the crowd of my peers who were smiling at Peter and smiling at me and if they thought anything was cosmic, they sure weren't saying it. Peter could do anything because he was popular. It was the Emperor's New Clothes all over again. I shuddered at the power of high-school hunks. I cringed as Peter floated up to me and reached out his stupid hand. I looked away. The music swelled, my stomach churned. He pulled me up from the folding chair and onto the dance floor, pressed me toward him, and flattened my corsage. The metaphor was too dim to ponder.

I was standing with Peter at the buffet table. He was close to drooling. Heather and the Heartbeats had taken a break to pull themselves together and spray their hair with liquid asphalt. I really prayed they'd be done spraying soon because break time was not good for Peter. It meant we had to talk.

I was moving him around the table so we wouldn't get stuck in any one place and have to have a meaningful conversation. He was still limping a bit from my kick in the shin, but nobody said love was easy. Everyone wanted to chat with us. I worked the crowd like a politician, saying nothing of substance, tossing pithy comments to my admirers while dragging Peter behind me. I tried to make eye contact with Trish, but she was huddled in the corner with Tucker, lost in love. She didn't care about me. I focused my thoughts on the waiting gold King of Hearts crown, which sat on a red velvet pillow at the base of Big Ben's sainted foot. I tried to picture it on Peter's head and what an honor it would be to be his date. I practiced smiling benevolently like females do from floats and things when they are in the public eye and are expected to be everyone's ideal.

I smiled until my smile muscles hurt.

A lone kazoo blurted through the tumult. I turned with everyone else to see the King of Hearts Dance Committee parade down the dance floor in full regalia, holding a red velvet pillow upon which sat a large, leering papier-mâché cupid.

I froze in time.

It had dark mocking eyes, its head was bigger than its body. Its wings were made of pink crepe paper, its bow and arrow formed with Reynolds Wrap. My larynx closed, my heart gave up. Gary Quark put the cupid on a waiting string and hoisted it over the dance floor, where it twirled like an ominous storm cloud. Becca Loadstrom said, "Oh, it's cute."

"Are you mad?" I shrieked. *"That is a cupid!"*

Everyone took a step back and said yep, it sure was.

The cupid twirled above my head. Peter reached out to me. Deep inside, the truth hit my soul like a Scud missile.

I was a fake!

It rang in my ears, it sizzled in my brain.

Fake! Fake!

I looked at all the glittering girls who hadn't gotten here by cheating. I tried to remember that all's fair in love and war. But the cupid just hung there, leering at me, reminding me of what I'd done.

Gary Quark said we'd start lining up for the King of Hearts announcement in a few minutes. Peter started toward the empty mike on the stage like he had something wildly important to say that needed amplification. I blocked his path.

"I have to say it, A.J.," he protested, "I—"

I shoved my hand over his mouth like the little Dutch boy who stuck his finger in the leaking dike to save his town from the rising flood waters. It was going to be a really long evening, as they say in Holland.

Leaks were bursting out everywhere. I was hurling sand-bags along the riverbank to push back the rampaging tides. Peter tried to read me the poem he'd written, the poem that began:

> I think that I shall never say
> A name as lovely as A.J.

I emitted a scream and ripped the poem into minuscule threads that could never be reconnected. I stormed to the buffet table, where I ate myself into oblivion in a last-minute attempt to hit all major cholesterol groups before I had my nervous breakdown. I stared at the papier-mâché cupid.

I had to contact him.

I wrote pithy emergency phrases on pink napkins (GO GET JONATHAN and HELP ME, I'M LOSING IT) and held them up subtly to the papier-mâché cupid, but he hung there, unfeeling, unmoved.

I shut my eyes and heard the somber bleat of the kazoo signaling to the world that It Was Time.

I was slumped on the spiral staircase with Peter and the rest of the court awaiting the drum roll and Gary Quark's ultimate announcement of the Winner. The staircase seemed shaky, particularly the center section, where Peter and I had been placed. Popular people know how to stand on a questionable staircase unafraid. When you're a fake, you feel every wobble. I listed to the left and gripped the rail, figuring I could crash down the steps between Al Costanzo and Mike Griswald in case tragedy struck. Nowhere is it written that you have to go down with the ship if you are only dating the captain.

Everyone below was looking at all of us above. Most of the Court took this in stride, because they were used to fawning adoration, except for Barry Lund, who everybody liked but who wouldn't win because he was not hunk material—he was token nice-guy material. I wanted to take my vote back and give it to Barry, but when you are a public persona, you have to ride your stupid, life-destroying mistakes full-speed across the finish line with everybody watching. I said we were all going to die, as the staircase wobbled and everyone else kept smiling except me.

Finally, the moment was upon us. Gary Quark sidled up to the microphone really slow to draw out the anticipation.

Silence enveloped the Student Center.

Gary blew a final, soulful squawk on his kazoo and motioned for a drum roll. He held up the hermetically sealed envelope that had been kept under lock and key in his father's disaster-proof safe since Thursday. Deenie

Valassis inched toward the staircase holding the Crown and yanking up her dress strap.

"The winner . . ." Gary announced loudly, ripping the envelope open.

". . . and this year's King of Hearts . . ."

Deenie waited . . .

"Peter Terris!"

Shouts and applause rose from the dance floor as Deenie crowned Peter, who lowered his head like he'd expected it all along. I tried to shake his hand in congratulations, but he scooped me up and hugged me with undying affection. The other members of the Court and their dates turned to shake his hand, smiles frozen in place, although in reality they all wanted to trip him. I grinned extra hard at Lisa Shooty, whose fake smile was melting. Peter was beaming and waving and leading me down the staircase carefully to avoid early death. We promenaded before the whole glittering school, the Correct Couple of the Century, as the papier-mâché cupid twirled above in mythological harassment. Red, white, and pink helium balloons were released to the ceiling, several of them getting stuck in the rafters to test Ned the janitor's patience Monday morning.

Peter kept saying he couldn't believe it as people tore toward us. Everyone said they had voted for him; everyone shouted congratulations to me.

I haven't done anything, I wanted to cry. *I'm just dating royalty!*

Gary motioned Peter and me onto the dance floor. I tried to feel the magic, tried to rekindle a paltry flame, I tried to get into it for the glory of the Crown, but my sin was ever before me.

Gary said, "Ladies and gentlemen, I present to you *your* King of Hearts!"

"*And this,*" Peter shouted to his subjects near and far, "*is my queen!*"

It was simply too bleak. I lowered my head and considered abdication, but when you're stuck with a half-crazed monarch, the only thing you can hope for is peasant revolt, and these peasants were ecstatic.

The applause rose greater. Peter looked at me with blind love. Penitence thundered through my soul—I'd destroyed a life! I wanted to tell him how very, very sorry I was, but Heather and the Heartbeats started singing and Peter and I had to dance. I fought back tears; the weightiness of forever crashed over me. I looked up at the papier-mâché cupid who leered down from the ceiling.

"I love you!" Peter cried.

"No, you don't!" I shouted. "You're confused!"

"I'm not confused," he said, twirling me.

"Yes, you are! You just think you love me, Peter! *You don't!* You don't care anything about my photography, you don't care about my hopes and dreams!"

"*I love you!*" he shouted blindly.

"*I don't want this!*" I wailed.

"And what, my friend," said a familiar voice, "do you want?"

I jolted erect. It couldn't be . . .

The flutter of dinky wings filled my ears.

But it was!

I gazed in consummate wonder as Jonathan flitted down from the rotating Valentine heart and swept past the papier-mâché cupid, casually eating a grape like it was no big deal. He fixed me with a steely glare.

"Jonathan!" I cried.

Peter looked at me strangely. "I'm Peter," he said.

I said of course he was.

"Who's Jonathan?" he demanded.

Jonathan was flitting like a butterfly, his puny wings beating in irritation. I couldn't think.

"Who's Jonathan?" Peter demanded, grabbing my shoulder.

I pushed him away.

Jonathan buzzed in my face and waved me toward the bathroom. "Step into my office, my friend."

"Yes!" I shouted, and flung myself toward the ladies' room.

CHAPTER FIFTEEN

I was sitting in a locked toilet stall, which nicely defined the moment. Jonathan was perched on a toilet-paper roll, looking smug. I grabbed my head that was pounding, I grabbed my throat that was closing.

"Oh, Jonathan, I thought I'd never see you again!"

He watched me somberly.

"I'll do anything you say! Just please zap me out of this nightmare!"

He crossed his teeny legs. "I did warn you of the consequences, my friend."

"Oh, you did, Jonathan, and I was so *pathetically stupid*!"

"You deceived yourself," he said firmly.

I nodded wildly in agreement.

"But your journey, my friend, has brought you this far."

"Frozen in time in a locked toilet stall . . ."

"You must not," he said, "confuse where you are with what you are to become."

"I've made the Ultimate Mistake in the Universe, Jonathan! I hate what I've done! I've ruined my life and forced Peter Terris into an awful, controlling mold and we will always be miserable unless you do something because I can never love him!"

Jonathan adjusted his bow and arrow slowly.

I flailed my arms: *"Save me!"*

He fluttered and stood on the toilet-paper dispenser, looking downright majestic, which is a pretty good trick when you're six inches tall.

"This is the moment, Allison Jean McCreary, where, if you let it, the truth will come."

Warmth shot through me. I didn't try to shake it off. *"All right!"* I shrieked. *"Let it come!"*

I expected something of a meteor shower. What I got was a cupid edict. "Remove Peter Terris from the dance floor and meet me at the Benjamin Franklin statue in five minutes."

186

"Why?"

Jonathan glared at me. Steam rose from his hot pink ears. "Do it!" he ordered, and zoomed off.

Heather and the Heartbeats were singing their extravaganza slow dance medley, "Great Makeout Songs of Yesteryear," turning the entire dance into a pulsating Hormone-O-Rama. Peter was draped around me; I was trying to pull him toward Big Ben. Jonathan was fixing his arrow in place, impervious to my plight.

His *arrow*!

He was going to shoot Peter again!

Explosive energy thundered through me. I yanked Peter across the dance floor to Big Ben's saintly foot.

"Stay there!" I ordered him, and turned to Jonathan sweetly.

"You're late," he said.

He zipped over and handed me my F2 like it was a lethal weapon.

"You will need this, my friend."

Peter was grinning at me, hugging me, exploding in waves of royal ecstasy.

Jonathan flitted back. "You must keep him still! If he moves, the arrow might not penetrate."

"Freeze!" I shrieked at Peter.

He didn't. He hugged me and laughed. I yanked his hands to his side. "Don't move!" But he did.

"I can't stay still around you," Peter declared, grabbing me.

"This won't do," Jonathan announced. "We are running out of time!"

"Then *you* keep him still!"

"Keep who still?" Peter asked.

I said I didn't know. A crowd of students were heading toward us. Jonathan fluttered his wings and sent them back to the dance floor. "It is now or never, Allison Jean McCreary!"

I felt the weight of my beloved F2.

"Peter, I want to take your picture!"

"Nah . . ."

"I'm taking it!" I shoved him into place to the left of the King of Hearts poster in a nice pyramid configuration off Big Ben's bronzed boot. Peter looked around, embarrassed, and shook his sandy hair. I crashed down on one knee to get an upturned angle.

"Don't move!" I pleaded.

Peter half smiled like the Mona Lisa. I snapped and snapped again. Jonathan fixed the arrow in place, raised the bow to shooting position, and held the grip loosely to face his target.

I was clicking like crazy now, moving around Peter, catching the fine features of his right profile. I said we were almost through, just hold it a tad longer. Peter moved to the right. Jonathan waited. I shouted that this was no joke, he had to stay *still*!

Peter froze in place.

Jonathan pulled back the arrow.

I focused the F2 on Peter's face.

Jonathan released the arrow. It whooshed cleanly through the air and sliced through Peter's heart with a final, pulsating *thwonk*.

Peter didn't flinch.

"Are we through?" Peter asked innocently.

I said I really hoped so.

Nothing happened.

Jonathan remained in shoot position, waiting. A cold emptiness gripped me.

Jonathan flitted over to peer into Peter's eyes and pull the arrow out of his heart. He hovered in his face, watching . . .

Peter shook his head. He rolled it to the left, to the right.

"Listen," Peter said, "instead of going to Lisa's after this, how about we . . ."

I sank to my knees. It hadn't taken . . .

"Weird. . . ," Peter said. "You know that pain in my chest? It just went away."

His love-drenched eyes grew hard.

Peter Terris squared his manly shoulders in utter irritation. *"Are we through yet?"*

"Perfect hit," Jonathan said proudly.

I lowered my camera. "We're through."

We're through.

I thought it would have felt different than it did. I

thought I would have shouted something in frenzied celebration. I thought at the very least that a great freeing breeze would clear my mind and cleanse my life from the ravages of oppressive love.

None of this happened.

I just felt cold—raw, shivery cold—the kind you get when you're walking in a freezing rain that won't let up and your whole body turns to slush. I guess this was how maturity felt—dreary, senseless, unfair. I'd hoped for better, hoped that when the time finally came growing up would have been worth the fight. Maybe if he didn't hate me so much . . .

We're through.

I sifted the words and the enormity of them didn't register. Peter Terris brushed off his tux and adjusted his crown. He asked if I'd seen Julia. I said I hadn't been looking. He said, "Gotta go," with consummate indifference. I watched him walk away through the crowd, free, unencumbered. He shook his sandy hair and raced onto the dance floor to get away from me.

Welcome back, Peter, to the Land of the Insensitive Hunk.

I leaned against Big Ben's base like a popped balloon. Jonathan flitted toward me, beaming. He was going to congratulate me on being mature—a state of being, I felt, that was highly overrated.

I got up and slumped off, past the stage, past Peter and Julia Hart, who were dancing so close that you couldn't tell where one of them started and the other began, past the mob of ardorous students swaying slowly on the dance floor, clutching and nuzzling in Valentine schmaltz.

Everybody had somebody except me.

Heather announced that it was time for the King's dance and would the King and his date come up front and lead the way?

Peter pulled Julia up front with him as the entire school stared at me in stunned silence. You have no claim to the throne when you're only dating royalty. I caught my haggard reflection in the melting ice heart on the buffet table as the music began to play for everyone except me.

So this was it?

This was the Visitation?

Peter Terris turns back into a world-class chump and I, the unloved heroine, slump in the lonely tower.

Thank you, Jonathan, for absolutely nothing.

A throat cleared behind me. I turned around. It was Tucker Crawford standing there in a tux and a T-shirt and his SAVE THE WHALES button, extending his hand.

I stiffened. *"What?"*

"Wanna dance?"

I stared at his outstretched hand and didn't take it.

He motioned to the corner where Trish Beckman had one high heel off and was rubbing her foot dramatically so that all could see how deeply she was in pain, how she couldn't possibly dance.

"How come her foot hurts all of a sudden?" I demanded.

"Because," Tucker said evenly, "she's your best friend."

I took his hand.

We walked onto the dance floor. People parted for us the way they do for people in wheelchairs when they roll by. I could see why Tucker hated to dance—he was awful at it. Peter was fawning all over Julia. Tucker stepped on my foot. He said he was sorry he wasn't better at this. I said he was just fine, it was almost over. Then Gary Quark cut in on him to dance with me; Tucker left, relieved. Gary said he really liked my dress; I laughed and said his lime-green tux was perfect. Then Barry Lund cut in on Gary and Al Costanzo cut in on Barry, and the music kept going and I kept dancing with guy after guy and found myself face to face with Robbie Oldsberg, who said he was sorry about our little misunderstanding of last year. Could we go out again sometime?

I said "No, thanks."

The words flowed out without hesitation or remorse.

I said it again.

"I heard you the first time," he grumbled.

A rush of energy zapped through me. I smiled

from deep within as Peter and Julia tripped the light fantastic. I danced two fast dances with David Voorheese, Julia's date, who didn't have my mature mythological perspective. I jumped and shimmered and twirled and glistened and then I danced with Carl Yolanta—two dances, nice and slow—but DeeDee Fenton, his date, was turning consummate crimson on the sidelines. I pushed Carl back to her side. I danced half a dance with Bobby Pershing and the other half with Nick Savalas, and when it was over, I didn't want to dance anymore.

I turned to walk away to find Jonathan hovering over me like a dinky helicopter, holding my F2.

"There is much more to see, my friend."

He lowered the camera into my hands.

I held it, and as I did, power shot through me like lighting zapping a rod. I shook out my hair and spun around to face the dance floor.

I focused on Peter and Julia. They were dancing cheek to cheek and I didn't feel lonely when I saw them through the viewfinder. I caught them in the frenzy of lights and blur so that their faces were hardly recognizable and snapped. Peter's crown slipped off his head and I caught that in midspill, blurring the background elements so that just the crown and his hand trying to grab it were emphasized in the Ultimate Royal Statement. I used the wide-angle lens to shoot through the lub-dub heart to catch the dancing couples. I tilted the camera to an unsettling angle and caught Heather and the Heart-beats singing off center. I moved to the middle of the dance floor and everyone got out of my way. I shot the rotating Valentine heart in a mad rush to highlight the twinkling effect. I isolated my silhouette against the stage in a searing self-portrait. I caught the melting ice heart on the buffet table in a stunning commentary on the end of things just as a flash of moonlight drifted over the scene.

I knew at that instant why artists have to suffer: It's the only way to see beneath the surface sometimes to the truth below.

I ran to the stage just as one side of the WHEN TWO HEARTS BEAT AS ONE banner drooped to the floor. I lay on my back and shot it From Below to give it bigger-than-life perspective.

Pearly Shoemaker walked up to me. "Think *prom,* A.J. There's always a bright tomorrow."

"I can't think about the prom now, Pearly."

She held out her hand to help me up. "I understand perfectly; there's been a death here. You need to get over it. Go through all the stages of disgust, anger, disillusionment. But you'll come out a better person, A.J., because no matter what happened between you and Peter, you have made your mark and no one can take that away from you: you got the best boy in school to fall in love with you!"

"He's a dolt, Pearly."

"We're talking concept, A.J."

I hung my F2 over my shoulder. "It's the wrong concept."

Couples drifted toward the parking lot. Heather's voice cracked on the last song. Trish and Tucker offered me a ride home, which was extremely decent. We walked arm in arm through the lub-dub heart that was making high-pitched squeaking noises. Roger Dexter kicked the side and told everyone the squeaking was not his fault—it was Manny Pontrain's fault for buying cheap transistors at Radio Shack. Tucker said when you cut corners, you always pay.

We made it to the bleak cold of the parking lot just in time to see Heidi Morganthaller toss her wine cooler aside and throw up on Jeff Dintsman. Trish said she'd never seen me look better as we climbed into Tucker's pickup and rolled through the ice and slush toward home. I knew without question that I had just taken the best photographs of my life.

CHAPTER SIXTEEN

You wonder how parents cope at all through the teenage years, how persons of supreme middle age don't have more seizures than they do. Take my parents. They're sturdy people. You have to be sturdy to stand in a hallway and not lose it as your only daughter swings home from a dance *not* with the boy she left with, but with her best friend and her date, sashays through the front door completely alone and in charge of her life and her art, and says with supreme cool, "Mom, Dad, how was your evening?"

My parents froze in dumbfounded silence.

I said that I'd just taken the photographs of a lifetime, I wasn't tired at all, I was energized with life-giving creative emancipation. I grinned at Dad when I said it because I knew he'd understand.

"Park it!" Dad croaked.

Mom put her hand gently on his shoulder to calm him down. I sat purposefully on the blue corduroy couch where I could get good and depressed better than anywhere, but depression was far from me.

"Speak!" Dad ordered.

Stieglitz barked. I told him he was a good dog. I said, "Peter and I called it quits and I'm perfectly fine. He was the wrong guy for me. We live and learn."

Dad opened his mouth but nothing came out.

I told my parents the whole mind-bending story, except the part about Jonathan. I wasn't ready to tell anyone about that yet. I went into massive detail about the anointing of consummate creative power and the feeling of supreme control that only a person who is going to make it in her chosen field could *ever* experience. I looked at my father the whole time I said it. Mom was smiling, lit from within, because she felt this way when she made Beef Wellington. Dad was watching me like he was trying to figure out a complex puzzle.

I said, "Well, I guess I have some film to develop." I headed up the stairs with Stieglitz at my heels. Dad followed silently behind.

. . .

The darkroom has a different attraction for every photographer. For me it's the quiet. So much of the creative process whirls around chaos, but in the darkroom I never speak a word until I'm finished, out of respect for the work being born. It was something Dad taught me.

I had just fastened a wet contact sheet onto my clothesline to dry. I shone a flashlight over it, searching the boxes of small photo squares for the best shots to develop.

"*Wow*," Dad said quietly.

My heart leapt with pride. I picked four standout shots—the crown, the blurred dancing, the melting ice heart, my silhouette against the stage. I'd connected tonight. The feeling was everywhere I turned, in every move I made. I exposed them with the enlarger while Dad sat on a folding chair, watching. I sloshed the photographic paper in developer solution as one by one the hazy images bled into sharpness. They were superb. I squeegied each one and hung the wet prints on the clothesline to dry. Dad's expert eyes studied each shot checking for shadows, distortions . . .

"Amazing. These shots have power, A.J."

Dad's face got soft. "I owe you an apology." He leaned against the gray supply cabinet we'd rescued four years ago at the dump. "I've made a big mistake and I need to make it right."

I sat on a folding chair and half missed the seat.

"When I left filmmaking," Dad began quietly, "I

felt like a failure. I was hurt and angry because too many people had said no to my work. I vowed that I would never work at anything again that didn't have a regular paycheck attached to it. I've kept that promise to myself and it was the right decision for me. But I also vowed that no daughter of mine was ever going to suffer like I had."

I looked down, studied my ankle, and said I'd suffered plenty.

Dad scrutinized my dance prints like they were the Dead Sea Scrolls. "I was going to make sure that you had a career with absolute security," he continued. "In my mind photography didn't qualify. I didn't want you to watch a dream die like I had to."

He let out an antique sigh. "When you showed such talent for photography I was excited and scared. And then when you got so good at it I was downright . . ."

Dad walked toward me. I was looking down like a little kid and only saw his Nikes. He planted them square before me. "I had no right to track your life, A.J., to decide who you could or couldn't be."

I looked up to his knees, his chest. He extended his hand. "Can you ever forgive me, honey?"

I looked at my father's hand that was reaching out to me.

I looked at my father's face. It was filled with remorse and sadness.

I didn't want to cry, but my eyes were misting. Dad took my hand. "I'm very sorry, honey. I really believe, A.J., that you've got the talent to make it."

The words didn't register at first.

"Really?" I cried.

"Without question."

I clung happily to his hand. My eyes filled with tears.

"I'm sorry, too, Dad. I knew you were hurting, but I couldn't see beyond my hurt to yours. You were just trying to protect me—I know that now. You spent all those years teaching me photography . . . I'll never be able to thank you enough."

Dad walked toward my dance prints. Their glory beamed through the darkroom like a searchlight cutting through fog.

"I bet on you," he said.

Well, you know how it is when you've been waiting for an important person to give you the nod. Your hope soars into space like a cupid zooming toward the moon. I stood there looking at Dad and we started laughing and connecting because my art was so tied to his that sometimes I couldn't tell where one of us started and the other began. I can't remember who started hugging who first, but it was unquestionably the best hug I'd ever had, because it was a hug of all-out acceptance.

"This does not," Dad warned, "mean that you just

approach this whole thing like some wafty airhead. You have to think about how to support yourself, about how you're going to make it happen."

"I will, Dad."

"I wasn't as consistent with that as I should have been, A.J. Every artist needs something to get them through the lean times."

"I have you, Dad."

"Always," he said. "Just get a day job, kid."

It was so late, I was beyond caring. Dad and I were at the kitchen table scarfing down steak sandwiches with sautéed peppers.

Dad patted his mouth with a napkin. "I learned something about myself tonight," he said. "I finally figured out why I didn't make it with my art."

I stole a Frito off his plate. I'd finished mine. "Why?"

He leaned back in his chair and smiled sadly. "I wanted to be a filmmaker, A.J., because I liked the thought of it. But I wasn't good at many of the things you need to be good at. I hated pushing one long project for months and years at a time. I hated the personal and financial sacrifices. I was terrified in the free-lance world every day, wondering if I could earn enough money to live on. The films I really enjoyed doing were the short funny ones, not the long ones with meaning."

He laughed. "You know, advertising is a good place for a guy like me. I get a paycheck. I use my filmmaking to create short, punchy spots. I make people laugh. I've got security." He ate a Frito and frowned. "I've also got dancing cereal chunks up to my earlobes. This ChocoChunks account is making me crazy . . ."

"You could get another client, Dad."

He nodded. "And I'm going to, honey. I need to start working with a product that's good for people again."

Dad cut two gargantuan slices of Mom's Triple Fudge Blackout Cake and plopped one on my plate. "Which reminds me," he said, "now that we're getting really serious"—Dad took out a piece of paper—"I jotted this down while you were gone tonight. Just a few thoughts to remember from your old man."

His eyes got soft as he began to read. "I hope, A.J., that as you mature as a photographer, you will always appreciate the constantly changing gift of light. I hope that you will know a community of artists that can sustain you, that your desire for your art will grow stronger, that criticism will make you stretch and go beyond yourself, and that you won't ever be afraid to put your butt on the line. I wish for you a sensitive soul that cries when things hurt and an eye that sees beneath the surface to the humor hiding in difficult moments. I hope that you take risks and never care about using too much film—toss it off, roll after roll—it will only make you better. Film is impossible to waste. And I hope that your work will always speak to someone about who you are—if you can accomplish that, it will last long after both us are gone."

I was overcome. "You wrote that tonight?"

"Yep." He folded the paper.

"It's beautiful, Dad."

"First draft too."

I beamed. "But you hadn't seen the dance shots yet . . ."

"Nope. But I've seen everything else you've ever taken." He handed me the paper.

It was early morning, after five. I was sitting on my purple Persian floor pillow still holding the paper Dad had given me. I'd almost memorized it by now. But something else was happening, something appalling. Jonathan was packing up his quiver.

"You can't," I shouted, "be serious!"

He put the last arrow and two tiny apples inside and laced it shut. "I must leave you, my friend. My work is truly finished now."

"Your work isn't finished! I'm still a social wreck! The only male who nuzzles me is Stieglitz!"

Stieglitz heard his name and tried to climb into my lap.

"It is the only way, my friend. I cannot stay with you in this form forever."

"What if I crash and burn?" This was likely.

"I have great faith that you will not."

He turned to face me, his eyes warm and kind. "Your emotion is your strength," he said. "To feel things deeply is a precious gift."

"I won't . . . see you again?"

He smiled. "You will see me often, Allison Jean McCreary, but differently."

"I don't want you any different!"

He fixed me with a mythological stare. There was no stopping him.

"I want to know what happened, Jonathan . . . with you and that other teenager . . ."

His little eyes grew old and sad. He sat next to me on the pillow. "I will tell you, my friend, since our time is drawing to a close." He shut his eyes, seeking strength. "I could not make her trust me."

"Why not?"

"She so wanted to be loved, she was so afraid of being alone, that she was willing to stay in a false relationship with a young man who brought her unending sorrow. She would not trust her feelings. She would not trust me." He fingered his quiver. "I was brash and impatient with her. I left her too early in the process. I planned to come back and teach her a lesson, but I left before true trust had grown between us. When I returned, she had no foundation from which to believe in me or herself. My words rang hollow. She turned away."

"That's so sad . . ."

Jonathan sighed.

"But you left me, too, Jonathan. You were *really* impatient at times—no offense. I was ready to puree you in the blender . . ."

"I was," he agreed. "I am learning each day and trying to better myself. Impatience is a profound failing."

Tell me about it.

"Thankfully, beneath the anger, my friend, you believed." He fluttered up and hopped into my hand. "She could never believe enough to let go, and so the time of her Visitation ended. I had to leave her with the fulfillment of her wish."

I shuddered at the thought.

He patted his quiver gravely. "The choices we make can have lasting consequences." Jonathan looked around my studio, studying every corner, like he was trying to memorize it. Then he turned to face me and held up his hands. "But I have righted the wrong with your Visitation," he declared with power. "Thank you, my friend. I have found peace."

I gulped. "You should be celebrating, Jonathan . . ."

He smiled and extended his dinky hand. I took it. It was like the smallest baby's hand ever. "I will continue to carry that young woman as I will continue to carry you, Allison Jean McCreary—in my heart." His little hand fluttered by his heart and rested there, laying claim to what was inside.

"I'll carry you, too, Jonathan." I was crying now.

Dawn broke across the sky flooding my studio with early morning light.

"It is time, my friend."

I hung on.

"I wish I could have taken your picture, Jonathan . . ."

He shook his tiny head. "Some pictures are meant to live only in the heart, my friend."

The warm, familiar ooze started trickling through me. I had to let him go.

"All right," I said finally, "how does this work? Do you whoosh off on a rainbow, do we flag down a limo?"

He smiled like a little angel and flew to the black still-life pedestal. "Someday, Allison Jean McCreary, you will tell others what you have seen."

I cried all the harder; Stieglitz jumped up to comfort me. I whispered "Thank you" as Jonathan folded his wings, raised his puny hands to the ceiling, and began twirling like a top. He closed his eyes, threw back his tiny head, and like a photograph stilling a whirling moment in time, he was instantly transformed back into a Coney Island cupid doll with a tacky little sash and stuffing spilling from his cheek. He flopped down, a tiny love soldier who'd been wounded in battle.

The growing light illuminated his essence.

Then the cupid doll leaned a little to the left as Stieglitz and I sat silently and pondered the miracle.

EPILOGUE

I had just arranged Trish Beckman on the small wire chair on my front porch in the definitive psychological statement. I uncrossed her legs, tilted her head to the left, and checked my light-meter readings for shadows. This portrait was my birthday present to Trish, who was low on cash and needed something emotional to give to her parents on their twenty-first wedding anniversary. Trish maintained that no one could take her picture decently except me. This was true.

I had given the photo session total thought, at first

envisioning Trish painted black and blue in an avant-garde expression of psychotherapy with shades of Andy Warhol, but that is not the stuff that adorns family rooms. I opted for the classic, purposeful head shot that chokes parents up. I said the session had to be outside even though it was the end of March because Trish's cheek color peaked outdoors, giving her a ruddy air, an excellent statement for a budding therapist who will spend the next forty years inside on an upholstered chair listening to the world's problems.

I had gotten down on one knee for a Bigger Than Life Perspective when Trish recrossed her legs and said, "You've changed, A.J., do you know that?"

I raised my new Nikon that my father had given me for my eighteenth birthday, said I knew I had, and clicked.

"I mean," she continued as I moved to get her right side, "ever since the dance you've connected with yourself."

"Public humiliation does wonders for the soul," I said, kneeling now for another shot.

Trish's eyes grew moist and far away. She almost rose an inch taller in the chair. I clicked.

"It's like this presence is with you," she said. "I can't explain it."

I said, "Don't cross your legs," and shot her straight on, catching her head tilted just slightly in empathic listening. I grinned because I knew I had gotten a great one.

Dad had said the same thing to me.

It was right after he got off the ChocoChunks account and was put in charge of the new campaign at Gibbons natural yogurt, a product to be proud of that would make the world a better place and had annual sales meetings in Hawaii. "Something about you is put together now," he mused. "I can't quite put my finger on it."

Mom zeroed in on it too, right after she declared the unthinkable—that she was bone-tired sick of working so hard and had decided to take Sundays *and* Mondays off (possible retail suicide) and hire a part-time baker. "Being eighteen certainly agrees with you," she said. "But I think it's more than that."

It was.

Not that turning eighteen isn't a huge change in an individual's international scope, flooding the brain waves with cosmic wisdom. It was that I was alive to things as I'd never been before. My senses were heightened. I laughed more; I cried more. My camera sizzled in my hands. I took nothing at face value—there was always more to see—I watched life, studied it, from a new plane. I was hungry for truth.

I was experimenting feverishly with early morning light, getting up before dawn to set up at ponds, the beach, to catch the first streaks of dawn flashing across the sky. I appreciated the morning so much more now. It was the time of day when life seemed to shout the most promise and I wanted to capture as much of it as I could. I found a family of ducks nesting one morning by the Crestport River and I squatted there in the high grass for hours, holding my Nikon, my thigh muscles spasming, waiting for the stupid mother duck to get it together and do something momentous. She pushed her babies into the water like a drill sergeant taming new recruits and I caught every moment.

I'd also developed a keen appreciation for things that flit. Insects, birds—I was fascinated by wings of any size—I burned off rolls of film getting some absolute knockout shots while trying to capture the miracle of flight.

It's funny the things you remember.

I could see Jonathan so clearly at times—his dinky expressions, his bow and arrow, his epic irritation when he'd really had it with me—then at other times my memory would fade and I'd look at the cupid doll on the still-life pedestal and ask myself if any of it really happened. I'd pick up the doll and shake it and shout "I know you're in there, Jonathan!" And I'd lug him around with me in my ace camera bag fully expecting him to burst through the stuffing anytime, leading a tall, gangly male who would love me forever so I wouldn't have to be hurled into the dating oblivion of the summer before college, also known as the Black Hole.

Stieglitz missed Jonathan too, and once dragged the doll off for two entire days without my permission. I went ballistic searching for the cupid, finally finding him underneath the basement steps on Stieglitz's stash of half-eaten bones and mangy slippers, lying there like a small dead thing. I scooped the doll up.

"Bad dog!" I screeched at Stieglitz, who whined pathetically, convicted of his sin. Stieglitz climbed into my lap and pawed the doll gently.

"Oh, Stieglitz, I miss him too!"

We sat there for the longest time, fully expecting another Visitation because we needed it so badly. But we got nothing for our efforts. Not one measly flit.

Dad was working out his funny spots for Gibbons natural yogurt, having great fun creating yogurt containers that could hit baseballs out of the park and sing opera—"real naturals," as the slogan went. Dad played arias through the house as he bonded to his yogurt vision, free from the shackles of children's breakfast cereal.

Mom was working hard to Rest, but change comes hard to middle-aged people. The first Sunday morning she took off, Mom got up early and made Dad and me German apple pancakes instead of sleeping in. Around ten she entered Blind Panic, convinced that all her customers would flee to other markets when they caught wind of the part-time baker. Mom threw on her sunglasses and drove slowly past all the nearby gourmet markets, straining to see if any of her customers had gone AWOL. After a month of this, when she realized her business wasn't headed for the toilet, Mom learned to sleep until six on Sunday morning. Her goal was to snooze until nine and not make breakfast. Sonia suggested we hide her car keys on Saturday nights just in case.

Peter and Julia had broken up twice since the dance. The last time she threw a lime Sno-Kone in his face after he whistled at a St. Ignatius cheerleader in epic lust. I got a stop-action shot of the throw in midhurl. It was anybody's bet if they'd make the prom.

My King of Hearts Dance shots hung in the Student Center, shouting a warning to all who drew near to look beneath the surface of life's experiences to the truth below. I was hot at work on what could become the definitive statement on senior year—"Overcoming Inertia," a photographic study of tired students getting up from their desks. Carl Yolanta posed for me, although there was nothing inert about him. I liked the way he looked when his shoulders slumped and he pushed his glasses down on his nose. I liked the way he looked in general—he had kind brown eyes, soft brown hair, and an excellent neck. He's a consummate backpacker— really into the earth. When he told me he was a morning person, I laughed and said I was becoming one too. We took an early morning walk in the woods last Saturday, hiked down to the narrow part of the Crestport River, stood in the high grass, and fed breadcrumbs to the squirrels. Then Carl said the nicest thing to me: "I've wanted to get to know you for a long time, A.J., because I always liked your photographs. You can tell a lot about a person by the pictures they take."

I smiled supremely all the way to and from Trish's, having just presented her with two searing eight-by-ten portraits of herself, guaranteed to make her parents cough up extra spending money when she left for college. She and Tucker were becoming quite the item, and Trish was in psychological heaven probing the deep recesses of Tucker's wounded inner child. I didn't feel any sense of urgency to tell her what Carl had said. I just drove home, massively content. Trish and I would always be there for one another no matter what. That was the unspoken pledge between us.

Pilling Pond had melted. When it froze again, I'd be at college. I got accepted at NYU *and* Rhode Island Institute of Design, two superb arts colleges, in the same week. Isn't that just like the educational system, to throw in a multiple choice test when they think you're not looking?

But I was ready.

Amid the tumult and the pain I'd discovered a secret: People can misunderstand your vision, they can try to change it, but if you've got the fire, they can't douse the flame.

Truth is a funny thing—once you get used to it, it usually sets you up for more. I was sitting at Pilling

Pond right by the TULIPS RESTING/DO NOT DISTURB sign, my Nikon in my lap. The overhead clouds had just parted for the warming sun when I felt a dripping in my heart, and the familiar warm ooze washed over me, laying claim to what was inside. I was propelled up by the sheer power of it and raced down the street as Stieglitz careened ecstatically at my side. I tore past the Crestport Savings and Loan, tore past a little kid who was making a historic mudball, adding brown muck to it, thrilling as the weapon grew bigger in his hands. Not every photographer would kneel down on a dirty street in March to get a shot, but when you're going for the essence of a thing, you've got to shoot it right, no matter what. I shot the kid From Below to heighten the moment and got up quickly when he turned to me, brought his arm back, grinning . . .

"*Don't,*" I ordered, "*even think about it, kid!*"

He threw the mudball at a pigeon. I brushed myself off. Photography is a dangerous passion, *not* for the fainthearted.

I started running again and the ooze kept dripping as Jonathan fluttered in the deep places of my heart. I was flying by the seat of my designer jeans; Stieglitz was at my heels. I passed a really cute guy in a metallic-blue jacket and gave him only a fleeting glance because there's a lot more to life then genetic perfection. A blue mist broke through the gray sky, unleashing streams of pure sunshine, and I knew that Jonathan was watching me. He was there like a little sunbeam brightening everything I did.

I flopped on the steps of Petrocelli's Poultry and lifted my face to the warm, filtered light.

Maturity sure has its moments.